William Wetmore Story

A Poet's portfolio

Later Readings

William Wetmore Story

A Poet's portfolio
Later Readings

ISBN/EAN: 9783337156268

Printed in Europe, USA, Canada, Australia, Japan

Cover: Foto ©Andreas Hilbeck / pixelio.de

More available books at **www.hansebooks.com**

A POET'S PORTFOLIO

LATER READINGS

BY

WILLIAM WETMORE STORY
D. C. L. (OXON.)
K. C. C. I., OFF. LEG. D'HONNEUR, ETC.

BOSTON AND NEW YORK
HOUGHTON, MIFFLIN AND COMPANY
The Riverside Press, Cambridge
1894

A POET'S PORTFOLIO

LATER READINGS

He. Oh, is that you? I am delighted to see you. This is a totally unexpected pleasure. I had no idea that you were in these regions. When did you arrive, and where are you staying?

She. I arrived only yesterday, and am staying at the same place; at that little old farm-house, you know, where I put up when I was here three years ago. It is very primitive and unpretentious, but it is clean; and the people are so kindly, and in every way it was so pleasant to me there, that I thought I would return and spend a month here again. But I am quite as much surprised to find you here as you can possibly be to find me. I had no idea that you were in these regions. I thought you had gone to Switzerland.

He. I did have a half plan to go there, but after wavering for some time, I finally decided to return here. I had some literary work to do ; and here it is quiet and peaceful, and one is beyond the range of tourists, that throng in Switzerland and buzz about everywhere like flies. There is not a nook or corner or peak or valley that is not filled with eager crowds of pleasure - seekers, and where one can really find peace. So, knowing that here at least I should find rest and solitude, I determined to return to this place.

She. And what, may I ask, is this literary work that you have laid out, — a poem, a novel, a romance, a history, or what ?

He. "Be innocent of the knowledge, till you approve the deed," as Macbeth said to his " dearest chuck."

She. Dearest chuck, indeed! A queer sort of a dearest chuck was Lady Macbeth, was she not ? But whatever *she* was, your " deed," I hope, will be different from his ; or do you intend to murder some other literary man with the dagger of your pen ?

He. Oh ! You wish to be an accessory before the fact, do you ?

She. Perhaps.

He. Oh, no ! Where ignorance is bliss, 't is folly, you know, to be wise.

She. You are always quoting, as usual.

He. It is a vice of mine, I admit, but an innocent one after all; so you must forgive me. Do our best, the world has always been before us in all our thoughts and doings and sayings, and it is pleasant to hook one's self on to some famous predecessor who has said our best things before us. Nevertheless, you know, " Pereant isti qui nostra ante nos dixerunt."

She. No, I don't know anything of the kind. I can forgive you for quoting, so long as your quotation is of something familiar, but when you come to quoting old Latin tags I cannot forgive you; and to take advantage of me in that way is neither fair nor friendly.

He. I will try to be fair, and certainly I will be friendly. But you are standing. Won't you take a seat on this mossy bank ?

She. I thank you. Yes, I will, for I have had a good long walk, and nothing could be more enchanting than this spot. It is as enchanting as it seemed to me in my memory, for if I do not mistake, it was here that we spent a long, pleasant morning some three years ago, when you read me a number of poems out of your sketch-book. You see, I have come back again to the same place, with no expectation, indeed, of seeing you here, but to renew the old memory of that delightful day ; for it was a delightful day, was it not ?

He. It was to me. As to whether it was to you, you best know. Of course you will say that it was.

She. Yes ; I say it was, because it was ; and more than that, you know it was. What could be pleasanter than to sit under the trees, and look out over this charming prospect, and hear this brook gurgling in its downward course over the moss-covered boulders, playing its delicate accompaniment to the poet's voice as he read his own poems ?

He. That depends very much upon who the poet is and what the poems are that he reads. To hear a real poet read his poems is delightful, I admit, always provided he reads them well. But I can conceive of nothing more tedious and irritating than to listen to a lot of commonplace verse, read by a commonplace poet, or so-called poet, who expects you to praise everything he reads.

She. But *that* every poet expects, or at least desires, whether he is a real poet, as you say, or not. But you must confess that I did dare to criticise much that you read, and I on my part will confess that you took all my criticisms in a kindly spirit, and now I expect just such another morning.

He. Oh! you do, do you?

She. Yes, I do! and if that does not imply a pretty compliment to you, I know not what will. But what are you mooning about now, — writing, drawing, dreaming, or what?

He. Well, I suppose "mooning" is about the best word to describe my present mood. I am doing what the trees and the flowers and the common people of the earth, that we call weeds, are doing. Growing, I hope, but at least submitting myself idly to all the strong influences of nature, and not bothering my head

with anything in particular, — not work-
ing, as we call it. The best things that
ever come to us come without our will.
They are gifts from who knows where.
So I am lying here fallow, ready to receive any seed that falls, weed or flower,
hoping that if anything comes, it may
prove to be a perfect flower, — that is, if
I hope for anything, for I am not ener-
getic enough to-day even to hope. To
hope is to seek, and to long, and I am
only idly mooning, —

She. And I come in to interrupt you,
like a stone thrown into a quiet pool of
water, and scare away all your dreams.
A horrible reality, am I not ?

He. Yes, a reality you are, and a dream,
too. But let me add that you are a
charming reality. I am truly delighted
to see you. What a wonderful hat that is
of yours. What an almost ideal dress,
so light and delicate in color. Really,
you might be, perhaps you are, a sylph of
the woods.

She. Nonsense ! Why do you talk
nonsense to me ?

He. You like it, — you know you do;
and was there ever a woman who did not

wish her dress above all things to be admired ? 1 know we men are very clumsy in expressing our admiration, and nearly if not quite always praise the wrong thing. We are far less clever than you of the other sex, who can talk for hours on the subject of dress, and show such knowledge and taste, and discuss with such warmth the tying of a bow, the folds of a skirt, the arrangement and color of a ribbon, or the trimming of a bonnet — I beg your pardon, I mean a hat.

She. Oh, if you are in this mood, I am going. Good-by.

He. No, you are not going away. On the contrary, you intend, and I applaud your intention, to sit down on this bank under the shadow of this great chestnut-tree, and have a good long talk.

She. And if I consent, what will you do to repay me for this expenditure of my most valuable time ?

He. Anything that you command.

She. Well, read me some more poems, or verses as you call them, and be pleasant as you were three years ago.

He. Ah ! how your sex do like to play upon the weaknesses of mine. With what subtle flatteries you lead us on to make fools of ourselves. No, I will not read you any more poems. I dare say you have made all sorts of fun to your intimate friends over my vanity in reading those little verses to you three years ago.

She. No; you think a little better than that of me. Confess!

He. Well, at least, you had a few little private laughs at my expense, did you not? Confess!

She. I confess nothing of the kind. On the contrary, if I have to confess, honestly, though I don't like to flatter you, I have kept in my memory some of those poems you read, and often tried to recall the very words. But memory is treacherous, and I am afraid the words have gone. But the sentiment, the thought, the feeling and movement still remain, and I should like to hear them all over again.

He. Oh, dear me! no, no, and no again! Don't disturb a pleasant memory; the vaguer it is, the better.

She. Please read me some new ones, then.

He. No; nothing can ever be repeated

without loss of its original charm. Better to leave things alone. No original impression of anything connected with a deep feeling can ever be renewed. The second time has never the charm of the first. In this life one never can have both hands full. We return to the old places full of hope and sentiment, but alas! the somewhat that enchanted them once has almost always, yes always, gone. The Hesperian apples turn to dust in the hand that grasps them. Do you remember that exquisite morning in June when we sailed together in our yacht, with the fresh breeze swelling our sails, and the sea breathing its salt odors and gleaming in the sun, a few snowy clouds slowly drifting across the blue sky, the white gulls dipping at intervals into the sea and rising again with heavy sickle-curved wings, to sweep away into the distance, and we were a happy company, lounging on deck and talking and laughing and singing? How enchanting it was! So enchanting, that we did nothing but talk of it for weeks and months, and we would have it again. Oh! we must have it again. There was no dissentient voice. So the same happy company (you were one, you know) chose what they thought a delightful day, and set forth on their sail, and the early hours were very pleasant, not quite so pleasant in fact as they had been in memory, but very pleasant, despite some little drawbacks. Somehow or other, the hours did not sing and rhyme as they did before. We had forgotten that September is not June, and when we were out in full sea, suddenly a huge black cloud lifted itself from the horizon and swooped down on us, and the thunder roared, and the lightning flashed, tearing its fierce seams in the clouds; and then came the rain, as if it had never rained before, driving us down into the cabin, and the laughter began to be a little spasmodic, and what began in hope and joy ended in experience. Don't you remember?

She. I remember nothing of the kind. It is all an invention of yours. What I remember was the direct opposite. The first day we had forgotten the biscuit — or was it the marmalade? and just because we had forgotten it, every one wanted it, and longed for it. But the second time we remembered it ; and the day was perfect, and it was ten times as pleasant as the first.

He. We all of us long for what we have not ; that is natural, necessary, universal. I remember a little boy and his mother whom I once met at Newport. They occupied, at breakfast, the next table to me. The boy was willful and out of humor, and the mother, the light of whose life was evidently the little boy, tried in vain to tempt his appetite by offering him this and that delicacy, anything that she could think of, and the boy always sullenly refused her offers. At last she cried out, almost in despair, " Well, darling, what will you have ? " " Just what you ain't got ! " he answered. We are all of us like that little boy. We sit at the Banquet of Nature, who offers us everything that heart could desire; and we turn peevishly away, and cry out for something impossible that cannot be given.

She. As for Nature's offering us everything, I deny it. There is no such harsh stepmother as she is ; nearly everything we long for and pray for she denies, and pelts us with misfortunes. Even her bonbons have very frequently stones in them. Sometimes, I admit, she is in good humor and gives what we crave, but this is very rare. Ordinarily she is harsh and cruel, and only jeers and laughs at us ; and then she is so capricious, — to-day all smiles, and to-morrow all threats and blows. Offers us everything that heart could desire? Yes, I think so. She may offer them to you. She gives you poems, — those are her best of bonbons, — but to me what does she give ?

He. Charm, beauty, a happy heart, and a beautiful dress, and art to wear it with grace. Your hat itself is a poem, with those soft feathers that look as if they had come from a cherub's wing. Where did you get it ?

She. Please don't talk nonsense, but read me something, won't you?

He. I thought I was making myself very agreeable. Don't you think I show a good deal of ability in my description of your hat ?

She. Do say something serious ; read me a serious poem.

He. Oh, well, when you assume that tone there is nothing left for me to do but to sacrifice myself ; and here is a really serious poem, which I call "The Bride dressed for the Ball."

She. Now I know it's going to be ridiculous. The very name is enough. But I suppose I shall have to hear it.

He. Brace your mind to it. It is a little sad, perhaps, but things in life are so sad.

She. Oh, then, it is a serious poem.

He. Very, very sad, and here it is.

Do I look well ?   How do you like this
    dress ?
Charming ? Enchanting ? Oh !
Really I *am* so pleased. You like it ?
    Yes ?
I think it's pretty, too.

She. There ! I knew it would be some nonsense like that. But go on, since you have begun.

He.

I've put the diamond necklace on, you
    see !
And on my breast, see ! here

Are those sweet flowers you brought to-
day to me.
One kiss for them ?   Yes, dear !

Be careful, do be careful, oh, I say, —
See how you 've crushed those flowers.

She. No, on the whole I don't care
about hearing any more of those verses.
I knew they would be very foolish from
the very title you gave them, and so did
you, Fritz, did not you ?   That bark of
yours was very expressive, and you don't
like them, do you, darling ; and we won't
hear them, will we ?

He. Ah, that is Fritz's opinion, is it ?
Then there is nothing to be said if he dis-
approves.   Well, well, my dear little
friend, you shall have your way.   I won't
read any more of those verses, since you
do insist ;   I won't, indeed.   Come and
be friends !   How well he looks ; what a
beautiful Dachshund he is !   But you
don't care for him, I suppose.

She. Care for him !   I adore him.   I
don't think life would be worth having
without him.   You are a perfect blessing,
are you not, dear little Fritzzie.   I only

wish men were half as good, and half as honest and loyal and unselfish.

He. Oh, men ! They are the most contemptible things. Don't talk of men. Life would be so much better without them, would n't it, Fritz ? Only women are adorable, and I don't know what we should do without them, particularly when they do us the favor to come and sit on a mossy bank beside us and listen to our verses.

She. Did you ever have dogs of your own ? If you did, you know what a gap they fill in one's life ; how beyond all words they are loyal in their friendships. One may entrust to them one's secret thoughts, and they never gossip and report and talk scandal. One at least may be sure of one's dog, if not of one's human friends. Dogs have no ifs and buts in their love. There is no one who believes that I am all perfection as Fritz does. He forgives me for all my waywardness, for all my injustice to him, sympathizes with me in all my moods and variations of temper, is never angry or cross to me, but always kind and humble and faithful in his love, whatever hap-

pens.   Are n't you, you dear little Fritz ?
Just look at those eyes of his.

He. I have no doubt he is all that you
say.   I had a little Dachshund once myself who was very like him, and who was
all that you say of Fritz.   Poor little
thing ! he died in my arms.

She. Did you ever write any verses
about him ?   If so, pray let me hear
them.

He. Yes, I wrote a few ineffectual
lines, for honestly, to confess the truth, I
deeply mourned his loss.   I did all that
I could for him, but it was useless, and as
I said, he died in my arms.   Still, I can
never forget the fond, beseeching expression of his eyes as he looked up to me,
trustingly as we to an uncomprehended
power above, believing that I could, if I
only chose, cure him of his sufferings and
make him well by a word, and I all the
while so utterly helpless to assuage his
pain and to justify his faith.   I often ask
myself the unanswerable question, what
dogs imagine us to be, what kind of a
superior power we seem to them ; and,
on the whole, I am inclined to think that
to them we seem to be some all-powerful

and extraordinary kind of dog, with fac-
ulties beyond their understanding, but
still dogs, wonderful and mysterious in
all they are and do. At all events, that
is what we mortals, in our ignorance, do
with the Infinite power above us, giving
to God the sublimed characteristics of
man, physically as well as spiritually.
If we confess the truth, we represent him
to our senses as a venerable, long-bearded,
superhuman man, whose laws and decrees
may be swayed and altered by prayers.
And I am afraid those prayers are often
as unintelligible as the barking and
whining of dogs is to us, and as unrea-
sonable, too, in their vague demands. I
could not help asking myself, as I held
my poor little dying dog in my arms,
whether our hope and faith in the Higher
Power, as we shape that power to ourselves, was as unfounded as his was in me.

She. But still we must cling to that
faith, for otherwise how could we bear
the ills and sorrows of this life ?

He. As poor little Fritz did, I suppose.

She. No ; he never asked himself the
questions which torment our human spir-

its continually. His life's moment satisfied him. He looked forward to no future beyond. But do not let us enter into these unsolvable problems. Rather, read me what you wrote about him.

He. I had quite forgotten that I ever wrote these lines until the other day a friend to whom I had given them, and who was as great a lover of dogs as you, recalled them to me, and sent me a copy of them, and as you wish to hear them, here they are. I am afraid they ask questions which neither of us can answer.

All this long night thy sufferings I have
    seen,
Thy moans of pain have heard, thy pant-
    ing breath ;
Thy dim eyes asking what I could not
    give,
But humbly trustful in thy dumb, fond
    faith.

What hadst thou done that thou should
    suffer thus ?
Thy life was gentle, kind, affectionate,
Unselfish, innocent.   Did this avail
To avert from thee this cruel stroke of
    fate ?

Nothing ! and sadly as I gaze at thee,
All impotent to give thee help, I cry,
"Why was this suffering given thee to
     bear ? "
Ah, vain the question ! There is no reply.

Then I recall thy little sportive ways,
Thy leaps and barks of joy, thy trusting
     nose
Thrust in my hand, thy happiness to lie
Under my arm, and pressed against me
     close.

Grateful for everything, a smile, a nod,
A kindly word — humble, submissive,
     true,
Quick to forget injustice, blows, reproof,
And seeking but thy master's will to do.

Where on this earth among our human
     kind
Is to be found such pure, unselfish love ?
Such patience under wrongs, such faith,
     that looks
For no reward hereafter, or above.

If such there be, I know it not, for all
Even of the best their earthly duties do

In the great hope, beyond this passing
    world,
That our poor little servant never knew.

Ah, shall we say, in pride of heart and
    brain,
" This is the end of all, to such as he,"
While Death for *us* but opens the dark
    gate
Through which *we* pass to Immortality ?

She. Thank you.   Yes, that is all true.
He. It was all true of little Fritz.
That is all that I can say.   I did honestly
mourn for that little thing, though, to confess the truth, I am not an universal lover
of dogs, as I believe you are.   One's own
dog is one thing, but another person's dog
is but too often (don't frown at me) a
mere nuisance, and all the more because
the owner finds something wonderful in
all it does.   The barking of my own dog
is not always a pure satisfaction, but the
barking of another person's dog sets my
nerves all ajar.   In this I at least resem-
ble Goethe, if in nothing else, and I often
recall his lines on the subject.
    She. His lines !   What are they ?

He. Manche Töne sind mir verdrüss,
doch bleibet am meisten
Hundegebell mir verhasst, —
kläffend zerreist es mein Ohr.

She. Did Goethe write that? That lowers him very much in my opinion.

He. Well, you know one can't help one's nerves. They get the better of us, sometimes, you must admit, and he may, for all I know, have been a lover of dogs, or at least of some particular dog, despite his lines, which perhaps were written in a moment of irritated desperation. He may have written them after some such call as I made the other day on a lady, or perhaps I should rather say, a visit I paid, for we *pay* visits as we do debts and bills. But no! Now that I think of it, though in this little poem, or Elegy as he calls it, he makes a sentimental exception in favor of one special dog belonging to his " mädchen," whose bark heralded her approach, still that story about the poodle and " The Dog of Montargis " seems to prove that he had a general aversion, or at least a strong objection, to dogs.

She. What story? I never heard it. Please tell me.

He. It was this. Goethe, you know, was at one time the director of the Weimar Theatre, and the Grand Duke was anxious that a famous actor of the day, named Karstein, should be requested to perform there the well-known melodrama entitled " The Dog of Montargis," in which a poodle is brought upon the stage and plays a silent but necessary rôle in the piece. But Goethe would not hear of this. Strongly as the Grand Duke urged it, Goethe would not yield, and after the first rehearsal he sent in his resignation, saying he would have nothing to do with a theatre in which a dog was allowed to appear. Nor could he be induced to alter this determination, and resume his position as director.

She. But what harm did the poor dog do ?

He. He not only did no harm, but the play could not be performed without him. It was not, however, to the play itself, poor as it may have been, that Goethe objected, but solely to the introduction of the dog.

She. You were beginning to tell me a story about a call you made on a dog-loving friend.

He. Oh, there is no story, it was only an experience which Goethe's lines recalled to me. As I entered the room, four dogs sprang at me, yelling and barking and making (excuse the term) an infernal uproar. Besides being somewhat suspicious as to their intentions in regard to my legs and trousers, my brain was entirely confused by this reception, — by this expression of joy (for so she termed it) at again seeing me. "Dear little things," she exclaimed, "how glad they are to see you!" *I* only wished they had not been so glad, or had been able to find some pleasanter way to exhibit their delight. Stumbling along with rather hesitating footsteps, however, I found a seat at last, and tried to say something, but all our conversation was punctuated by constant and reiterated bursts of barking, which even she found it impossible to repress. Not that she made great endeavors to stop the horrid noise; on the contrary, it seemed rather to amuse her, and at intervals she would say, smiling down upon the dogs and patting their heads : "No, darling, no! You must not, really. It's very charming, all you say, but we are talking now, dear!" Are we, indeed? I kept asking myself. What is she saying? What am I saying? I don't hear anything but what the dogs are saying, and what that is I neither understand nor appreciate. So, after a half hour of this, I made my bow, shook hands nervously, smiled as far as I was capable of smiling, and came away, to confess the truth, with a somewhat perturbed temper.

She. Yes, I admit that was annoying. But human beings very often annoy us quite as much.

He. Very true, but not exactly in the same way, and then we do not quite love them for it.

She. We ought to love them, if we were real Christians, and to forgive them, too, for they are our enemies, and despitefully use us.

He. Oh! forgiving is easy enough, but loving is not so easy; nor in fact is hating — I mean, really hating. There is a long step from dislike, or the negative of like and the positive of hate. It requires so much energy of mind and purpose really to hate. There are very few persons capable of being what Dr. Johnson

called " good haters." But haters are
not generally very interesting creatures,
whereas lovers are most amusing to out-
siders ; and though you refused to hear
the verses I began about two of these
lovers, I am sure if you had allowed me
to read them, you would have smiled.
They are not, I admit, purely Greek, but
they are at least simple, natural, and
ingenuous.

She. Greek ? I should think not, judg-
ing from the beginning. Parisian, perhaps, but Greek ! ! !

He. She was so provokingly lovely,
you see, with all those diamonds, and
that quaintly becoming dress, and that
wonderful lace, and all. But perhaps
you would have insisted on hearing the
entire poem if you had known who she
was.

She. Who she was ! I know perfectly
well without your telling. She was nobody. She was a mere fiction.

He. No ! She was the most beautiful
of women. Everybody admired her.
She was so full of wit and talent and
kindness and sweetness and spirit, and,
what is best of all, of charm, which means
everything.

She. Really! And who was this paragon?

He. Your great - great - grandmother, and she was all that I say. Indeed, whose great-grandmother was not? I never heard any one speak of her great-great-grandmother, who does not vehemently insist that she was a celebrated beauty, and admired by all. Did you?

She. If I answer honestly, I never did.

He. Mine was, I know, a perfect beauty. She exactly corresponded to the description one of my young New England friends gave me of Effie, or Nannie, or Nellie, or Minnie — I don't remember which. When I asked her what sort of a girl Minnie or Nannie was, she exclaimed, with a burst of enthusiasm, "Why, she 's perfectly sweet and lovely, just as sweet and lovely as she can *be* (with a strong emphasis on the *be*). She 's simply splendid! She 's gorgeous! I never did, I give my word, I never did in all my life see anything even half so fascinating and exquisite," and my friend pronounced this last word accentuating strongly the second syllable.

She. That describes my ancestress in her youth exactly. She was simply exquisite.

He. We both had the loveliest of great-great-grandmothers. Indeed, the whole family without exception were remarkable for something or other, — for talent, for spirit, for beauty, for size, for strength, for abundance of hair. Every great-great-grandmother, when she let down her profusion of golden or brown or jet-black hair, could walk upon it, and it always curled or waved.

She. Yes! I never heard of a great-great-grandmother, and scarcely ever of a great-grandmother, who had straight hair. The further they are removed from us the more beautiful, rarely beautiful, they are. One's great-great-uncles were only noble, fine-looking men, and some were bald, but one's great-great-grandmothers! Ah, that is a different case. But if, as you say, that poem was written about her, and of course I shall not be so impolite as to question your statement, I should like to know what has become of those diamonds and that lace. Who has got them?

He. You have.

She. I have ? and where are they ?

He. In that chest in the attic, put away with all the precious things she left. Do you mean to say you have never looked into it and examined it ? I thought curiosity was one of the features of a woman's character. You must know they are there. That old chest, you know, with the brass hoops, in the northeast corner of the attic.

She. Oh ! I 'm so much obliged to you. I have often wondered where the diamond necklace that I ought to have was. I will look into the matter immediately, — that is, as soon as I return home. What I do know is that this interesting fact has been concealed from me, and I think it is shameful. Can't you tell me something more about my family, — I mean those that have gone ?

He. Oh, yes, certainly ; but you must have heard of that pathetic little incident that happened centuries ago to your great-grandfather's first wife. She was a charming little creature ; she lived only a year or two after her marriage, and then died very suddenly. This is the account I received from a friend who happened to be staying with her at the time, and accidentally, I suppose, it fell into rhyme : —

She was gazing into her mirror
  And returning her own sweet smiles,
And half persuading and charming herself
  With her pretty, innocent wiles.

When behind her she saw Death's shadow
  Silent and cold and blank,
And closing her eyes, with a startled
    shriek,
  Into his arms she sank.

She. Oh, what a horrible idea! It will haunt me whenever I look into the mirror. I am sorry you read it.

He. Things will happen so, you know. Death is always lying in lurk for us. Whom the gods love, it is said, die young; and our friend was young, and never knew the cares and struggles and pains that accompany even the happiest life. Better to go so, than to outlive one's self and one's youth, and to totter down the vale of old age, accompanied by sad remembrances and abandoned by hope, — of anything in this world, at least ; all the gladness of life, if not utterly gone, overshadowed, and our happiest memories ending in sighs.

She. Oh, no ! no ! not always. Old age is sometimes so charming, when the agitations of life are over, as it sits peaceful and serene with a gentle smile on its face, brooding pleasantly over the past, with gentle memories, and if not in utter satisfaction, at least in calm content. The old loves never entirely die, and the life afar off behind us has a gleam and a color that nothing can take away; like the lovely and delicate distances in the landscape, which are perhaps really, and when we are near them, rude and hard roads through an uninteresting country, but illuminated by the sun's last rays seem in the dying light to be like fairyland. Old Donne was right when he said, —

" No spring nor summer's beauty hath such grace
As I have seen on one autumnal face."

He. How do you know ? Not by expe-

rieuce, certainly. That is the way old
age in its best phase looks to us ; but to
old age itself, how does it look ? For instance, —

To crawl between earth and heaven
  A poor old broken thing ;
To say of all joys, I have known them,
  And they all have taken wing, —
'T is worse than vaiu to recall them,
  Recalling them is but pain,
What is goue is gone, and no wishing
  Will restore it to us again, —

This is terribly sad. I know it,
  But youth had its trials, too,
Vain longiugs, wild wishes, for fruit and
      flowers
  That never on life's tree grew.
Even love at its best had its shadows,
  Ambitiou fell dead, half-way ;
We hit our young feet and we stumbled,
  And hurt ourselves even in play.

Old age has at least one solace
  That wild youth never had :
Calm, quiet, peace, no vain longings,
  But memories sweet and glad.

The tempests of passion are over,
　　And if the desires that we knew
Have vanished ; so, also, have vanished
　　Its disappointments, too.

What ask you, then ?　What is bet-
　　ter
　　Than simple, plain content ?
'T is a staid old matron — I know it —
　　Not the maiden so turbulent,
So full of wild graces and fancies,
　　The torment and joy of my life ;
But she keeps my household tidy
　　With never a word of strife.

She. Ah, yes ; that 's an old man's view
of it.

He. Yes ; but I have the misfortune
of being only a man.

She. But not an old one yet.

He. Oh, yes, old enough ; everybody
is old enough after he is thirty.　Some
of the oldest fellows I know are only
about twenty-five.　One would think, to
see them, that they had known all the
experiences of life.　There are blighted
beings in abundance of about that age,
— Byronic creatures, with their collars

down and their necks open, who moan over themselves and their fate, to whom the world is but ashes and dust — and all because Nannie did not smile. Those are the old young fellows who are amusing to all the world but themselves. But the old fellows who play at being young are perhaps quite as amusing, who brush up the side locks of their thin hair and endeavor to conceal the bare plains of — let us call it the upper forehead, and who compliment so, and bow with such grace, and are so aristocratic and high-toned in all their ways. When it comes to the really old fellows, who acknowledge their years, and are even ready to brag of them, — ah! then the case is different. It is difficult to grow old gracefully, to accept quietly and with dignity the ravages of time, to make no pretenses either one way or another, and to enjoy what remains of life. There is nothing that makes us feel so old as suddenly, after long years of separation, to meet one of the friends of our youth and prime, — one of the reigning belles as they were called; or one of the beauties with whom we used to flirt; or an old schoolmate

with whom we once played, and whom
we have lost sight of since, the old girl
or boy-look gone from their faces and
figures, and in their place, hollow cheeks
and wrinkled brows, made by the claws
of Time.

She. And then, sad thought, there
comes to some,

> " The last sad scene of all
> That ends this strange eventful his-
>   tory,
> In second childishness and mere obli-
>   vion,
> Sans teeth, sans eyes, sans taste, sans
>   everything."

The good Lord preserve us from that !

He. I don't know that when old age
comes to such a pass, it is quite un-
happy. It is sad to look at, but it does
not feel or know enough to be sad in itself. It has no special desires, or hopes,
or regrets, so long as it does not suffer
bodily. What is worse to bear is old
age with gout, and rheumatism, and
pains, and desires impossible to satisfy,
and a consciousness of its own helpless

condition. But let us not think of that.
When joy has gone, and we remember
more than we hope, and look back with
a deep sigh of regret to what has gone,
we are all of us old, whatever years we
number. So long as we take delight in
life, we are young ; but the sad and
weary heart is always old.

The torrent whirls over rock and stone,
 Sparkling and never weary.
As I watch it alone, — ah ! so alone,
 With a heart that is sad and dreary,
So sad and sore for what is no more
 And will never know returning,
For the joy that has fled, for the hope
  that is dead,
 For the light that no longer is burn-
  ing.

I would that this day had passed away
 With its toil and pain and striving,
And that I was at rest 'neath the earth's
  cold breast, —
 For what is the use of living ?
For what are our joys and our loves and
  our hopes
 But bubbles on Time's swift river,

That a moment gleam on its hurrying
    stream,
  And then burst, and are gone forever.

She. Yes, yes ; the world is what we
make it, — bright and sunny, dark and
gloomy, passionate, violent, or calm and
serene, as we happen at the moment to
be. Love and joy enchant everything.
'T is the spirit in which we look at things
which gives them their color.

  He. Yes. Tonio, who was forty years
of age, walked by that same place on the
evening of that same day, and sat down
on the same knoll and dreamed.

  She. And what did he dream ?

  He. Well, something like this, for looking back even at the lost and gone is not
always sad : —

Nina, do you those days remember
  When, in the amber moonlight's glow,
Those blissful evenings of September,
  Beneath these hawthorn bushes low
  We sat, — some twenty years ago ?

Ah ! then we swore to love forever,
  In voices passionate and low ;

And Fate we dared our hearts to sever,
  For we were young, and loved, you
    know, —
But *that* was twenty years ago.

What pledges then to life were given,
  The crickets listening below ;
The great moon shining up in heaven
  While vow on vow we squandered so,
  With faith of twenty years ago.

But love and youth and fame and glory,
  So real then in all their glow,
Are now a dim-remembered story
  Of some divine and dreamlike show
  That passed us twenty years ago.

And half a fact, and half ideal,
  O'er memory's magic glass you go,
And o'er your head, but scarcely real,
  There shines a faint auroral glow, —
  The love of twenty years ago.

She. False, fickle, and poor-hearted
creature ! He never loved, that is plain.
Nina's life he spoilt, and you 'd better
write her history. It is sad enough, you
know.

He. No ! I know nothing of the kind.
The old passionate fervor of love died
away in his heart, and the old life in
hers, but there survived a warm affec-
tion, a tender feeling, a peaceful sentiment, which lasted till death. And in
his old age, he dedicated to her some
verses, in which he strove, however inade-
quately, to express his feelings. Would
you like to hear them ? I have them,
I think, here in my portfolio. Yes, here
they are.

She. Do read them.

He.

Since last we met, how many a long, long
    year
Hath flown away with ne'er returning
    flight.
And now your face brings back those
    days so dear
That glow in memory with unfading
    light.
We both are changed. Still in your face
    I see
That same sweet smile, those same
    sweet tones I hear,
Those same sweet ways that so enchanted
    me,

When we were young and glad, without a fear.

" Ah me!" you say, " changed, changed
indeed, old friend,
Nothing is now as once it used to be."
No ; age to you hath had the power to
lend
An added grace to those of memory,
A grace that only time and age can
bring,
A twilight grace that noon nor morn-
ing knows,
A tenderer charm, that comes when even-
ing's wing
Its softening shade across all nature
throws.

With laughter once we greeted every
day,
And now we greet it with a silent
sigh;
Yes ; we were once more thoughtless,
glad, and gay,
But were we happier in those days
gone by ?
Through memory's mists, half real and
half dream,

Seem they not sweeter than in fact
they were ?
As the steep cliffs of distant mountains
seen,
Their rude facts veiled in mysteries of
air.

(Our hopes are fewer, but are calmer
far ;
We ask for less, but we have gained
content —
No wild, high dreams our peaceful being jar,
Life is a simpler plain, with less extent.
We know at last that youth's rash
dreams were vain,
And o'er our lesser round we peaceful
go,
Taking what comes, and not with eager
strain
Striving for what life gives to none below.)

What though your hair is white — I like
it so !
Softer it seems, more delicate, and
rhymes

More truly to the tender soul I know
  Than those dark curls you wore in the
    old times.
Nay ! do not smile and shake your head,
    dear friend !
  'T is really so — I simply speak the
    truth.
Too old for flattery ? Ah ! but I pre-
    tend
  Old age can be even lovelier than
    youth.

You are bound up with all those olden
    days,
  Their joys and pains, their sorrows,
    cares, and dreams,
And o'er your head a silent aureole
    plays,
  Lit by the light of far memorial
    gleams.
We have grown old together; we can
    hear
  Through far-off time the bells of mem-
    ory ring,
Some sadly sweet, some joyous loud and
    clear,
  That of the past in sweet accordance
    sing.

She. Yes! If he really wrote those lines as you say he did, I think I should have liked him better as an old man than as a young or middle-aged man. Time does not seem to have robbed his autumn fields of all the flowers of his young romance. There were still some scarlet poppies growing amid his ripe corn.

He. (Old age can be charming when it is honestly accepted by the owner. It has not so much trumpet and brass band as youth; but at twilight it can draw sweet pathetic tones out of the old harp or spinnet, that are sometimes very touching.) Did you ever read Cicero's treatise, De Senectute? There are some charming passages in it that I think would delight you ; and the sentiment throughout is most interesting, as well as its arguments for a future life, specially as coming from one to whom the Christian religion was unknown. One passage particularly struck me the other day as I was reading it ; it is in the last chapter, where he speaks of looking forward to a future life where he should meet all the great and good who have gone before him, and says that if any God should offer to make him young again, he would refuse the offer as having no charm for him.

She. Ay, but that, you know, was the offer that Mephistopheles made to Faust, and to accept which, old as he was, and philosopher as he was, he gladly abandoned all his studies, and all his researches in science. You see that he differed from Cicero.

He. Yes, I know he did. But in my opinion Cicero had the right of it. I never fully appreciated Goethe's scheme of the first part of Faust. As for the second part, it is not only inconsecutive, undeveloped, and almost, if not quite, unintelligible in its design and execution to all the world, but I fear even to the poet himself, for he seems throughout it to be wandering about in a mist, and not quite to understand and know his own way.

She. But what fault do you find with the first part? It always seemed to me most admirable and most interesting, and the work of a great genius.

He. Simply this: it seems to me that to an old philosopher, whose life had been given to science, to alchemy, to the most serious researches into life, in the hope to solve the secret which underlies all things, the mere offer of youth would have been but a poor and insufficient temptation to induce him to abandon all his studies and sacrifice all his hopes for the future. To sell one's soul merely to be young again, and to sell it for such a boon, does not, to my mind, accord with the character of Faust as it is drawn in the prologue ; and to such a devil as Mephistopheles is represented to be, a mocking, sneering, grinning fiend, with his silly cock's plumes, seems to make the discord still greater. Had the devil offered to teach him the infinite secret, to open to him the Book of Knowledge and interpret the laws of the universe, however futile and deceptive might be his promise, I can understand the lure and the reward. But simply to make him young again seems to me to be no adequate bribe. And, besides, is it to be supposed that Faust, the philosopher and alchemist, would have been for a moment satisfied, or even aroused, by the silly pranks of Mephistopheles ; for what, in fact, did that sneering spirit do for Faust to compensate him for the loss of his soul ? He introduced him to Auerbach's cellar, where he made jets of wine spring from the table. Then he carried him to the witches' company on the Brocken, who had nothing to tell him, and then presented him to a young peasant girl, whom, altogether at variance with all his previous character, he seduced and ruined. Is it possible that any old philosopher should have been willing to forego all the longings and studies of his life for such a miserable result ? No wonder Faust rebelled at times. One would think that any reasonable and decent person would have been disgusted at such impotent and vulgar results. But this philosopher, despite his casual rebellions, always yielded at last to the foolish persuasions of a low-minded, sneering spirit.

She. There is something, I admit, in what you say. I never thought of it in that way. But still, you must allow that all men, even the wisest, are waylaid by the evil spirit, that sneers at all that is high and good, and does seduce them from the high paths into low and base courses, and though they find in reality that vice does not pay, they still adhere to it.   You remember the old lines,—

" I see the right, and I approve it too,
Condemn the wrong, and yet the wrong
    pursue."

But why don't you, since you take these views, so contrary to the almost universal acceptance of this great poem and play, write one yourself embodying your own conception ?

He. Well, to confess the truth, I have written a few verses on this subject in which, while accepting the original character of Faust as the philosopher, I have endeavored in my small way to embody what I suppose his answer would be to such propositions and from such a spirit as Goethe's Mephistopheles.   I suppose him to be deeply engaged in his studies, when the sneering spirit makes his entrance and offers him his panacea of youth.   I see I have quoted as its heading that short passage from Cicero of which I spoke, in which he says, —

" Si quid Deus mihi largiatur ut ex hoc ætate repueriscam, valde recusem."

No ! sneering tempter, naught from you
    I ask
That you can give. You promise youth
    alone,
And its seductive joys. I know them
    well,
And I refuse them, even had you
    power
To give them back to me. It is not
    youth,
Though *that* was sweet, that I desire.
    Far more —
'T is knowledge that I crave, — the power
    to see
Into the inner world of life and things ;
Into the mystery that surrounds us all ;
Into the future, when this life is done ;
Why we are here, and why the power
    above,
Around, in everything that lives and
    moves,
Has placed us here, if death ends all at
    last.

All my long years' exploring I have
    sought
To read life's riddle, — not alone in man,
In all, from lowest things that creep the
    earth

To man, the highest here we see and
    know ;
Have sought the laws that rule the world
    of things
As well as living, moving creatures here ;
Sought them in science, alchemy, books,
    art, —
In every way that seemed to promise
    light,
Combining, analyzing, peering close
Into the parts of this material world
To seek their essence, and with lifted
    eyes
Holding mute converse with the silent
    stars, —
Guessing and reasoning, groping after
    light,
Fired by the hope that I at last might
    find
Life's secret ; and now here you capering
    come
With smirking and grimace, to offer —
    what ?
The boon of youth ; to make me young
    again,
To gratify man's lower passions here !
Wine — woman — all the human senses
    crave,

As if these satisfied the soul's desires.
Fool ! off with you into the lower world ;
Even this is far too good and high for
     you
With that ridiculous costume and cock's
     plume.
Off ! off ! I say.   Your offers tempt me
     not.

Tell me the secret of the life beyond ;
Tell me the secret even of this world ;
What death is, and what life is, — I will
     hear.
Tempt fools, that is your office, not the
     wise
Who seek for higher things, scorn all
     you say,
And all you are and offer in this world.

You 'll make me young again, you say,
     and I
With Cato, and with Cicero respond,
Even if a God should offer this to me,
And not a devil with his treacherous
     wiles
As you are, — I with them would say,
     No ! no !
Here in this life I am but as a guest,

A traveler resting at a wayside inn,
Longing to reach my home, not to turn
back.
My race is nearly run here in this life ;
I seek the final, not the starting goal.

Life is but toil and penance at the best.
The higher power hath planted in the
soul
Desires and longings that outreach this
world
Whose joys are transient, and whose
knowledge naught.
My hope looks forward to a wider
sphere,
Where all the good and great of yore
have gone ;
Where I may meet them, listen to them,
share
Their noble thinking with a larger sense,
A wider view ; where all the secrets
dark
Of this world here will be revealed to
me ;
Where calm in spirit, from base passions
free,
We may look down and see at last, and
know.

Here, the dark veil of death and doubt
    obscures
And overshadows all our life and
    thought;
There, all is clear. There, we shall see
    and know,
Not dream and hope and fear like trav-
    elers lost
In the dim darkness of an unseen way.
Why should I wish life's passions to re-
    new?
What *is* life at the best but toil and
    strife
And endless turmoil; a swift, turbid
    stream
Vexed by wild currents as it courses on
To the great ocean where it tends and
    ends?
And youth, what is it but a passing
    breeze,
A song that but a moment lasts; a dream
Haunted by hopes even while it lasts;
    a joy
That while we own it is not truly ours;
A gift that most is prized when it is
    gone?
Why should I ask to have my youth
    again

With all its passions, all its wild de-
    sires ?
No ! no ! in looking back our youth
    seems sweet,
But sweeter far in memory than in fact ;
For memory with its spell enchants the
    past,
And lends the sternest distances a charm,
But age looks forward to a higher life.

But ah ! why talk to you on themes like
    this,
Poor taunting devil ! Had you any
    shame,
Any belief, hope, faith in higher things
You had not dared to offer unto me,
Seeking for life and knowledge, your
    mean gift.
And so avaunt, poor fool ! Out of my
    sight !
My dim, weak candle shows but little
    light,
But purer light at least on life's dark
    path.

There, that is somewhat the kind of
answer that I should have supposed
Faust would have made, had he been an

old philosopher, and earnest student and seeker.

She. Almost thou persuadest me to agree with thee. But, if Faust had rejected the temptation, there would have been an end of it. There would have been no play at all, and that would have been an irreparable loss, would it not?

He. Not necessarily. Mephisto might have tempted him in another and more satisfactory way.

She. What way?

He. Oh, I am not going to be tempted to think out here on the spot the plan for a play, even though the tempter be so wise and so fair. And perhaps it is not a little presumptuous in me to criticise such a work as this of Goethe, which the universal world has accepted as a work of genius. But we have been led away a little too far from the subject of which we were talking, and I should rather go back to that. Let me see, what was it we were saying?

She. We were talking about old age, and when it really began; and you were saying that it is not so much a question of years as of feeling; and we were tracing it from the old young men through the young old men down to the last stage of imbecility and childishness.

He. Oh, yes, I remember ; and I was saying that sad, even terrible, as it was when it arrived to this, — at least to all friends and acquaintances and mere lookers-on, — it was not necessarily sad to the person himself, unless it was accompanied with bodily sufferings. It was, in fact, a second childishness, untormented by self-consciousness and impossible desires.

She. Well, don't let us think of that last sad condition. I don't wish even to forecast the possibility of such a state of things. Read me something a little brighter, if you please.

He. I send you to Cicero, if you really wish to read and ponder the thoughts and imaginings of a noble old man, filled with high aspirations.

She. I will read his treatise, certainly, as you so strongly advise. But now for something a little lighter in character.

He. Well, then, let us take our middle-aged man, who still is strong and well, but knows he is growing old, the more 's

the pity. He returns to his old home
and old friends after long years abroad,
which he has spent in amassing a fortune;
but he has never been married, never
been in love since the old days, the perfume of which still hangs about him as
he sees the old friends and the old places,
and hears the old voices. It is far away,
but still it is not utterly gone, and at one
of the first parties he goes to after his
return Nannie is pointed out to him.

Ah, no ! no ! It cannot be ! No !
   What ! that little stout figure, so gray,
Is the Nannie I once used to know,
   So brilliant and charming and gay,
So full of wild fancy and whim,
   So careless, so fair, and so young,
With a figure so slight and so slim,
   And a jest evermore on her tongue ?

And yet, now I look at her face,
   There is something I see in it still
Of the beauty she had, and the grace,
   And the loveliness, too, if you will.
There is still the sweet charm that
      entranced,
   And the same pleasant smile and sweet
      tone

That she had when we flirted and danced
  In the jolly young days that are gone.

'T is years, such long years, since we met,
  And I 've changed so ! Perhaps she
    will say,
Who is this old fellow ? And yet,
  Though I 'm older than she and more
    gray,
Perhaps she 'll remember me still
  And the days of our twenties. By
    Jove !
I will try it, and laugh if you will,
  But *she* won't, I hope, — my old love.

She. But you know she did laugh, and
smiled, and they grasped each other cor-
dially by the hand ; and he said, " I hope
you are well. It 's so many years since
we met, — some twenty, I fear. But
you look the same as ever." " Oh
dear ! " she answered, " I am afraid not,"
and she sighed, and there was a little
embarrassed silence for a moment ; and
then she said, " I hope life has gone well
with you, that — that you are happy —
and — well." And then Jones, the ubi-
quitous Jones, came up and interrupted
them, and spoilt everything.

He. As usual. There is always an intolerable Jones, who *will* come in with a laugh when tears are just brimming into the eyes, when the heart and soul are touched by some tender thought, some pathetic feeling. But don't let us be sentimental !

She. Oh, yes, let us be as sentimental as we can be. Have n't you any moans over the past that you have put into verse, and can read to me ?

He. Scores, I am sorry to say ; altogether too many.

She. Well, let me hear one. Do !

He. So be it, then. Our friend X. the unknown went wandering about the old places, and this was the result of one of his morning rambles under the shadows of the trees in *the* old place. There is always some old place which is *the* old Place.

Ay ! this is the place where I used to
    wander,
  In the happy days that are gone,
And dream of the future, while Hope on
    tiptoe
Beckoned, and lured me on.

All seems the same, though the trees
  must be larger,
 For nothing that lives is still ;
But in Memory's fond exaggeration
 The space is far larger they fill.

All things in life grow dimmer and
  smaller
 The farther from childhood we stray.
How boundless once seemed Youth's
  petty garden !
 How almost endless its day !
Time lingers with Youth and sports and
  dallies,
 But with Age it gallops fast,
And narrow to Age looks the little play-
  ground
 That to Childhood seemed so vast.

Here, as I listen, the far, old voices
 Call to me as in a dream,
And almost, for a moment, — alas ! but a
  moment, —
 A child again I seem.
The torrent among the moss - grown
  boulders,
 As it hurries gurgling along,

And eddies, and sparkles, and rushes, and
    lingers,
Still sings the same old song.

The voices of nature, the sounds, and the
    odors
Are still the same as they were ;
The hum of the insects, the birds in the
    shadows,
The whisperings in the air.
The wild flowers are blooming the same
    as ever,
And the quivering sunlight plays
On the waving trees and the spiring
    grasses
As it did in those early days.

But the thoughts and the dreams and the
    free, glad spirit,
The careless, unreasoning sense
Of a joy in mere living, that lent to all
    seeing
A feeling so glad and intense, —
Ah ! those have vanished beyond recall-
    ing,
And over the place is thrown
A silent shadow, a veil of sadness,
    A minor, pathetic tone.

'T is nothing the hand can touch ; 't is
  nothing
That eye, ear, tongue can tell ;
But a shadowy somewhat beyond ex-
  pressing,
Vague and intangible.
The very odors so faintly breathing
  Dim visions and memories bring,
And a ghostly feeling of something van-
  ished
  Hangs over everything.

It is not a definite sense of sorrow,
  It is not a real pain,
Nor even a pining desire and longing
  To have what is gone, again ;
There is something more dear in this
  unnamed feeling,
  That the spirit would shrink to give up
For the sharp, quick joy and the eager
  gladness
  That brimmed youth's sparkling cup.

So for an hour let me lie half-dreaming
  Under the blue sky's tent,
Softened and soothed by a peaceful
  feeling
  Of tenderest sentiment.

Not regretting and never forgetting
　The life that is past and gone,
But filled with a pensive sense of pleasure
　That gladness can never own.

After the early morning's splendor,
　After the radiant noon,
A tenderer sense steals over nature
　As the sun slopes slowly down.
As we sit in the twilight gray and tender,
　Is its shadowy light less dear
When we know that the work of the day
　　is over
And the stars are drawing near?

She. Yes, that's a little more serious
than some of the others, and I like it
better. Ah, me! the little garden *did*
seem so much more spacious when we
were children! I went last year back to
the old house where I was born, in that
delightful town of S., which charmed me
specially because the step of improve-
ment, as it is called, had but slightly in-
truded into it, and things, and places, and
houses were very much as they used to be.
Everything looked smaller, of course;
but, thank God, there was comparatively

little that was new there. The ghastly
new had not trodden over it and obliter-
ated the old. Even the ghosts were there,
and I communed with them sadly but
pleasantly; and the places I used to know
were sown with memories. Yes, even
the rosebush was still living that clung
about the porch, and the scent of those
roses had to my spirit something beyond
all saying.

He. Yes; I sympathize entirely with
you. There is nothing so associated with
memories of the past as odors. It came
over me the other day with peculiar
power. I was wandering about in the
garden at Ragatz, with no purpose, and
with nothing in my thoughts, when I saw
a single rose covered with the morning
dew, which seemed, as it were, to call to
me, as if it had something to say. What
it said I scribbled down at the moment
on the back of an old letter, and here
it is : —

I smelt of a rose in the morning,
    All cool with its sparkling dew,
So fresh, so fair, so fragrant,
    That it made me think of you.

It brought up the dreams of the old days
  Ere care and sorrow were ours,
And the dear old garden and shadowy
    trees,
  With its springtime fragrance of
  flowers.

And there again we were walking,
  And you were so glad and gay,
Laughing and talking, — and we were
    children,
  And life was a dream and a play.
The veriest nothings amused us,
  For everything seemed so fair,
And the simple joy of our innocence
  Was a perfume that filled the air.

It was but a little moment, —
  It passed, and I turned with a sigh
And wandered alone through the village
  And dreamed of the days gone by, —
Gone — gone — beyond all recalling;
  And a sad old man again
I wandered along, with tears in my eyes,
  Half of happiness, half of pain.

She. It is of no use to sigh and regret. Everything goes. Life is passed

either in looking back or in looking forward. Youth is always looking forward for something vague and indefinite, which it never grasps in its hand and really owns. And Age is always looking back, and trying to gather up the flowers that it carelessly dropped on its track, never knowing their value or enjoying their fragrance so long as it had them in its hand ; but when they are lost beyond recall, what a perfume beyond the telling they seem to have !

He. Yes, there is some truth in that, as well as in the opposite statement. It is vain to deny that we did enjoy our youth. If we could pick up those flowers again, perhaps they would not smell so sweet as they did when they were ours to own. Youth not only *seems* to us, as we look back, like a wonderful dream, it *was* a wonder and a delight in reality. We were not only young ourselves, but all the world was young, and new, and glad, and gay. The mere sense of living was a joy in itself, and out of its fountain ran for us a perpetual stream of delight, which waters the garden of dreams as long as life remains. And, by the way,

here are some verses which my friend X.
wrote, which perhaps may interest you,
as in some way illustrating what I was
saying.

She. Read them, please.

He. They embody only a man's feelings, as well as an artist's, and perhaps
you will not sympathize with them. Your
memories as a woman would naturally
be so different.

She. Read them, and don't make any
more apologies and explanations. You
know what pleasure it gives me.

He. Well, here they are : —

Oh, the gladness, the wild, careless mad-
    ness,
    That youth and youth only can own !
Oh, the joy of mere movement, the body's
    Free Carnival, — mere life alone
Being joy in itself, — the wild nature
    Asserting itself in our veins,
The blood mantling fast, the heart
    beating,
    The muscles' fierce struggles and
    strain !

All these once were mine, — the free
    gallop,

The wind blowing fresh on my face ;
The hunter's wild revel, the topping of
     fences,
The eager, glad zest of the chase ;
The tramp o'er the moor through the
     heather,
     Where hide the gray grouse ; the long
     stalk
On hills, hollows, rocks, — crouching,
     crawling,
     Scarce daring in whispers to talk,

But pointing, with gesture explaining
     Far more than with words, while we
     hide
And watch the far stag as he browses,
     And track him along the hillside
As he slowly moves on, ever watchful
     And lifting his head now and then
With a sudden and startled half-question
     And doubt of the presence of men.

Ah, then the mere stretch of the muscles,
     The straining and playing at strife ;
The wrestling, the racing, the cricket,
     the football,
     Were joys in the revel of life.
From study and wearisome plodding
     We slipped swift and scornful away,

For the body cried, — Come, leave your
    working !
There is nothing on earth good but
    play !

And now as above the low embers
    Of life I stretch out my cold hands,
And dream of the joys that have vanished,
    Before me a dim figure stands,
Who smiles, half in pity, and bending
    Towards me, I hear her lips say, —
It is true, both of body and spirit,
    The best man can do is half play.

So long as your work is mere labor
    The Gods will not smile nor approve.
In the highest and truest is hidden
    The germs both of joy and of love.
While your Art is mere toil and your
    goodness
Mere duty, 't is senseless and dead.
There 's a smile on the face of all angels
    And Beauty to Gladness is wed.

It is not enough in our doing
    To strive to do well ; all the while
We must feel in the doing and wooing
    A passionate joy, ere the smile

Of the Gods will be given.   Their blessing
  We only can win from above
When with glad and free spirit like
  children
We seek them in joy and in love.

She. My experiences are not, as you
say, exactly the same as those of your
friend X., but I do sympathize with him,
at all events, in the wild gallop over the
country.   That *is* fun.   Is n't it ?   That
is life.   As for the Art part of his verses,
it may be all very well, but I know
I had pretty hard work in trying my
hand at it, and I never succeeded in
doing anything worth doing.   I suppose
I did not work, as he says, in joy and in
love.   *That* I certainly did not, any more
than I did at my music.   Oh, how tedious those scales were !   But don't let us
speak of them.   Art, I think, in all its
forms requires very hard work.   I never
tried my hand at poems, or, as you would
say, verses, for I never could make any
lines to rhyme.   How do you do it ?

He. I know as little about it as you
do.   Where do any of our ideas and
thoughts come from, and why do they

take the form that they do ? And whence comes the moving force that impels us to do this or that ? Who knows ? Ah ! this is an entire mystery to us all. [The strings of the instrument have only the possibilities of music in them, and sometimes they are touched to tender tones, sometimes to harsh discords ; and sometimes they wait vainly for any touch at all, and are simply dead strings. And so it is with the spirit of man. All we can do is to keep it, as far as may be, in tune, and await, hoping that it may fitly respond when it is touched.]

She. When that power comes, — you call it inspiration, — you breathe it in as you do the air. Yes ; I understand the word, but it explains nothing to me, after all.

He. Can we explain anything, even the most trivial ? All life is in one sense a miracle. If I ask you, for example, the simple question how do you move your arm, can you explain ? It has at last become so familiar a fact in your experience, and it seems so simple, that it needs no explanation. But when you ask yourself really how you do it, you at once see that it is, like everything else, perfectly unintelligible. If this be so with the body, how far more impossible it is to explain the movements of the so-called spirit, — why it is affected in this way or that; what impels it; and in fact what sort of a definite idea have we of what the spirit is, as distinguished from the body?   And death, — what is death?

She. Ay, and for the matter of that, what is life?   We talk very glibly about these mysteries, but what do we know, — anything?

He. I have asked myself these questions so often, and the more I seek the less I know. Let me read you a few verses I wrote on this subject. Upon the whole, perhaps they are too serious to be in harmony with the day and the hour.

She. No; read them, please.

He. They were questions I asked of myself on the sudden death of a friend.

Gone?   What is gone? and where?
    Ah! who of us can say?
Somewhat, we know, that scarce an hour
    ago

Was with us here, quick, sentient, and
    aware,
Hath passed from Life away, —
What, where, we do not know.
Somewhat that lived and breathed and
    moved,
Thought, answered, reasoned, loved,
Hath vanished from us, out of sense and
    sight ;
    Gone like a breath into the air
    From this world's good and ill, and joy
    and care,
Unto the vast Unknown, the Infinite,
    Where human eye may vainly try
To track its pathless flight;
Gone, leaving silent, cold, dumb, dead,
The mortal tenement it habited.
The chambers all are here in which it
    dwelt,
Its windows open, — all that eye can see
Of its material house seems here to be ;
But what within it lived and moved and
    felt
Has gone forever, — whither, who can
    say ?
All that we know is something 's gone
    away
Beyond our reach, beyond our love or
    hate,

Where we too all shall go, or soon, or late,
And know what now is dim to us and
    blind, —
Beyond the reach and stretch of human
    mind,
Having alone the lights of Faith and Hope
With which into that vast beyond to
    grope.

Never again before me he will stand !
Never again the pressure of that hand !
Never again the gladsome light that
    shone
From those kind eyes ! Never the friendly
    tone
That used to greet me from those silent
    lips !
For Death hath shrouded now in dark
    eclipse
And wrapped in silence, terrible and
    grand,
All that I knew and loved, — nay, will
    not spare
The bodily vestment that Life used to
    wear,
But gives up even *that* to dark decay
Now that its human guest has passed
    away.

Gone to the land of spirits, — so we say.
What to do there? Will the long toil
    of years
While here he moved along this mortal
    way,
The experience, training, learning of this
    life
Gained by hard struggle, self-denial,
    strife,
Avail him aught within those spirit
    spheres?
Stripped of all life has given, what will
    remain
More than he owned when to this world
    he came,
A helpless infant? Must he there again
Begin a new life, struggle, toil, and strain,
And then beyond that life still onward go
To new existences without a name,
Where even our wildest dreams and
    hopes fall back
All broken-winged, incapable to track
One single step beyond this life below?

Where has he gone? Alas! we only
    know
That into the vague silence he has gone,
The dim, mysterious silence known to
    none,

From out of which he came, to which
    again,
All unaccompanied, he goes, alone —
To a new life, we say, we hope, we guess,
Or as fear dictates, to blank nothing-
    ness, —
The nothingness that was before his birth,
The dim unknown from which he came
    to earth.

And thus to end it all, perchance, were
    best, —
To pass into a deep, eternal rest,
Beyond the reach of human praise or
    blame ;
All toil, all trouble passed, all growth,
    all change,
All sad compunctions, all sharp pangs of
    shame ;
The soul swept far away beyond the
    range
Of personality and conscious sense
Into Nirvana's dreamless, blissful trance,
Beyond the reach of fate, and death, and
    chance.

Ah, this perchance were best, — no steps
    to climb,

No tasks to master, but a calm sublime
Man cannot know in such a world as this.
For, as Gautama says, Life's mystery is
In life itself inherent. Being here
All is illusion, — hope, joy, love, or fear.
End life, and all is bliss, for while we live
Nothing will satisfy. The soul will crave,
Do what we will, far more than it can
      have,
More than the cup can hold or life can
      give.

Yet, no ; the soul rebels against the
      thought
That it can ever end in vacant naught ;
That all the loves, joys, friendships,
      memories dear
That we have known and felt while living
      here,
When this life ends, and death's dark
      veil is drawn,
Will vanish utterly and disappear
And we be nothing, — a mere passing
      tone
On life's great instrument, that vibrates
      here
For one brief moment's space, and then
      is gone.

You are silent.

She. What is there to say ?   You have asked questions impossible to answer. You have held up a little farthing light to explore infinite worlds above and beyond, that are darkly hidden from us here.   And perhaps the best philosophy is to abstain from any attempts to explore into either the past behind our life, or the future beyond it, but without plaguing our minds with problems beyond our power, to resolve simply to strive to do our duty here as it comes to us day by day and hour by hour, to have a fixed faith that all that is is right, and to walk humbly through life.

He. Yes, undoubtedly ; but one cannot help asking such questions, futile as they are.   Still, I envy those who stretch themselves out on the pillow of the Church, and accept whatever their priest tells them as the word of God, and who satisfy their minds, or what they call their minds, by " We are told," — " It is affirmed."

She. Well, any faith is better than none.   The wisest as well as the foolishest know nothing.   But don't let us plague

our minds any more about such questions,
but go back to what you were saying
about our being instruments that Nature
plays upon, sometimes evoking harmonies,
sometimes discords and mere noises.
Have you any poem developing that
idea? If so, I should like to hear it, if
you will kindly read it.

He. Yes, here is one, I believe, which
touches upon it.

We receive, but we cannot create ;
   Thought is barren, and labor is vain.
Till the Gods give the seed and the sun
     and the rain,
   Nothing flowers ; and we humbly must
     wait,
Content if, from no one knows whence,
By the force of some influence
   Beyond all the reach of our powers,
Some seed shall be wafted below
In our being to blossom and grow
   And make what is sent to us ours.

Ah, what do our wishes avail,
   Or our strength that we boast, or our
     will,
Though we set to the wind every sail
   With the mariner's perfectest skill ?

What avails it ? Unless the wind blows
There we lie in a helpless repose,
  Or drift with no purpose, half dead ;
But when comes the breath and the blast,
The veriest rag on our mast
  Will give us a way and a head.

All we have, all we are, here, is given
  Or just for a moment lent ;
We are naught of ourselves, we must
    wait till from heaven
  That breath and that life has been sent.
We only can wait, and must watch
The impulse from heaven to catch
  With a spirit receptive and free.
Who can tell when that guest may
    arrive ?
Let it find us alert and alive
  To receive it whenever it be.

She. I dare say all that is very true in
its way. But you seem in this poem to
make very little account of the necessity
of labor and preparation on the part of the
receiver, be he poet, or artist, or musical
composer. Everything is to be given,
naught to be sought for or fought for,
or even deserved. I had no idea that

things came so easy as that. I thought a great deal of training and hard work was a necessary preliminary to any success in any form of art. But it would seem as if, like the beggars at the doors of churches, you artists had only to sit in the sunshine and stretch out your hands for alms.

He. Oh, you did, did you ?

She. So at least it would seem from your poem.

He. Oh, I see. You choose willfully to misunderstand it. Did I ever say that it was not necessary for an artist to work unweariedly and never to relax his efforts? Never ! But only that after he had done his best to prepare the way, the guest often does not arrive. Hard work is of course required, but that will not suffice if he has no ideas ; and where do ideas come from ? I suppose *you* know !

She. Of course I do, but I decline to tell you.

He. "This easy reading " is, as was once said, — excuse the profanity, but it lends force to the statement, — "d—d hard writing." This I do not understand to mean the mere writing in itself, that is easy enough, but the toil that has gone before, the hard hours of study and preparation.   And, by the way, there was once a young lady in Greece, I don't remember whether her name was Alsinoè or Phryne, but I am sure that she resembled you, for she was a most beautiful and interesting creature, just about your height and figure, as I remember her, though she did not wear the same dress.

She. Well, and what of her ?

He. I once overheard a little conversation she had with Phidias that I jotted down at the moment, without their knowledge of course, that may interest you in this connection.   It was this : —

Speak, Phidias ! speak, and say
    Does success wait ever on you ?
Have you never failed ?   Is your work
        all play ?
    Do you find nothing hard to do ?

Ah, my friend, every road that leads
    To the easy with hard begins ;
Nothing entirely succeeds,
    To Hope's goal nobody wins.

Hard ?   Of course it was hard !
  Failed ?   Yes, a thousand times !
Victory comes to the scarred,
  The heights unto him who climbs.

Through falling we learn to walk,
  Through failure to grow to power ;
And high on the topmost stalk
  Of Labor is Art's full flower.

Nature exacts strict pay,
  Nothing she lends or gives ;
No lingerer along Art's way
  The prize and the triumph achieves.

What we crave is beyond and before,
  What is done is behind and done.
The Future keeps promising more,
  And prompts us forever on.

The sternest of foes to the good
  Is the better, — the Best, the Ideal,
However 't is longed for, sought, wooed,
  Laughs fleeing away from the Real.

The labor in which we delight,
  The toil to which love is given,

Is the path that leads to Art's height,
    But the prize must come down from
    heaven.

There ; does that clear up the difficulty ?

She. I don't think there is much poetry in it, but it will do. " 'T is not so
deep as a well, nor so wide as a church
door ; but 't is enough, 't will serve," as
Mercutio has it. It 's very moral, I dare
say, and philosophical.

He. Sermoni propriora, I suppose you
mean, — " Properer for a sermon," as it
was once translated.

She. I don't understand Latin, and
you know it, but " properer for a sermon "
it certainly is. But I doubt whether it
is poetical.

He. " I do not know what ' poetical '
is : is it honest in deed and word ? is it a
true thing ? "

She. " No," Audrey, " for the truest
poetry is the most feigning."

He. You have n't praised a single one
of the verses that I have read to you.

She. Oh, you expected to be praised,
did you ? That 's singular, is n't it, for a
poet ?

He. Very, I suppose.

She. Why do you suppose I ask you to read them, and to continue to read them, if I don't like them ?

He. Oh, capriciousness, I dare say.

She. Thank you. Shall I begin to flatter you, and say that every one of the poems you have read to-day is perfectly exquisite ?

He. Yes ; you can say so, if you please.

She. And you will believe it ?

He. Ah, that's another thing. You know that I don't think any of these trifling things of any special value, but I read them because you command it, and I am your slave.

She. Well, don't let us skirmish any longer ; but go on and read something else. I cry out for more, — more, like Oliver Twist in Dickens's work. My appetite is not yet satisfied. No, really, honestly ! " I can suck melancholy out of a song " as well as Jaques, so " more, I prithee, more."

He. "My voice is ragged : I know I cannot please you."

She. Oh, if you will have Shakespeare, my answer is still that of Jaques : " I do

not desire you to please me ; I do desire you to sing. Come, more ; another
stanzo : call you 'em stanzos ? "

He. " What you will." But don't you
think we should better walk about a little
in the forest, and then we can come back
and read a little, if you so desire ?

She. No, I prefer to sit here. It is so
charming a place, and the brook sings a
perpetual silvery accompaniment to your
reading ; and I don't get a poet every
day. The great enemy to the good is the
better. Let us be satisfied as we are.
This is really an ideal place, a sort of
Forest of Arden ; and see ! there comes
one of the shepherdesses. How pictur-
esque she looks in her red bodice, as she
saunters along, with that colored kerchief
on her head. And what has she in
that basket, all covered with leaves ?

He. Strawberries, or raspberries, I
suppose. You know the woods here are
filled with them ; or perhaps she has
mushrooms. Oh, mushrooms, fit for the
tables of the gods, or to be tables themselves for Titania to feast on with Puck,
or Bottom, while she his amiable cheeks
did coy, and stuck musk-roses in his

sleek smooth head. Ah, buon giorno,
Livia. Che cosa hai lì nella tua canestra?
Lamponi? Fungi? Fravole?

Livia. Si, Signore, fravole. Guardi.

He. E quanto ne vuoi il kilo?

Livia. Quel che vuol Lei — Signore.

He. Ma dì — dì — quanto?

Livia. Quaranta centesimi, Signore.

He. They are strawberries ; would you
like some?

She. Oh, yes ; buy them all! What a
pretty girl she is! What a shy little
way she has, and what a sweet smile!
And such blue eyes! Is not that very
singular? I thought all Italians had
black eyes. And all these wild strawberries for forty centimes? It seems absurd, does n't it?

He. Every day there are scores of
these little peasant girls ransacking the
woods for strawberries, raspberries, and
mushrooms ; and they are up and at their
work long before the sun rises.

She. Poor little things! And what do
they do with them?

He. Carry them down to the neighbor-
ing villages, where they are bought and
sent to the city.

Livia. Addio, Signore. Grazie, sa.

He. Addio, Livia. A rivederci!

She. And who is this little girl? You seem to know her.

He. She is the daughter of one of the contadini here, and is a very good child.

She. She is very pretty and sweet and simple.

He. Ah, you should have seen her sister Fioretta, as we called her. She was really a beauty, and, young as she was, was a second mother to all her little sisters and brothers. Ah, me!

She. Why do you sigh, and say "Ah, me"? Did any misfortune happen to her?

He. I don't know whether it was a misfortune or not. Life is hard to the poor, and her family were very poor; and there were many mouths to feed, and there was little to do to gain the money necessary for even their small wants; and — but perhaps it is best as it was.

She. As what was?

He. That she should be taken away.

She. Who took her away, and why did they take her?

He. Oh, nothing peculiar happened,

other than what is always happening to
the rich and poor alike. I will read you
a few verses I wrote about her, which
will tell you her story.

FIORETTA.

She was but a peasant lass ;
    Nothing of the world she knew ;
'Neath the trees, along the grass,
    Like a wayside flower she grew.
Little thought or hope she had,
    Living happy for the day ;
Joyous, innocent, and glad,
    Life to her was only play.

Blue her eyes were, blonde her hair ;
    When she spoke to you she smiled
With a smile so shy and rare
    That the sternest it beguiled.
Fioretta she was named,
    For she seemed to one and all
Like a flower, — as unashamed,
    Modest, sweet, and natural.

So her little life of May
    Lived she all unconsciously,
Till it chanced, one summer's day,
    Death, as he came wandering by,

Paused, — and then with ruthless hand
  Plucked our little flower to bear
To a far-off better Land,
  Deeming her for ours too fair.

Now, whene'er that spot I pass
  Where Fioretta used to be,
Only a smooth mound of grass
  With a stone and name I see.
She is there no more to greet
  With a smile my seeking eyes,
And of all those meetings sweet
  Naught remains but memories.

She. Poor little Fioretta !

He. Yes, poor little Fioretta, so
pretty, so sweet, so gentle ! She is gone
the way we all must go. But, as I said,
it is perhaps better so. Who knows what
life might have brought her of pain and
sorrow and privation. She is safe from
all those pangs now, from all the slings
and arrows of outrageous fortune, and all
the whips and scorns of time, and all the
spurns that patient merit from the un-
worthy takes. Sometimes, when I am
low in spirits, I go up and sit by her little
grave. It is in a spot of consecrated

ground, overlooking (but alas! she does not see it) a vast and beautiful rolling country of hills and vales, thronged with trees, and bounded by a range of mountains that, veiled in blue mist, lift against the far-off sky. Through the valley, winding like a ribbon of silver, gleams the distant river, and on clear days sparkle the towers and dome and spires of the silent city that seems to sleep in its lap, all its noise and tumult and confusion of life shrouded and hushed in the distance. Now and then across the sky a falcon wings its way, sailing through the ocean of air with easy sweeps, beyond the reach of man's destructive wish. And here many a morning I sit and muse, and many a twilight I watch the sunset's dying glow, transfiguring the clouds that float above it with splendor, and gradually giving place to the still gray of evening. And there one morning I wrote some other lines, haunted by the memory of the little Fioretta. Shall I read them?

She. Do, please.

He.

> Whether it rains or shines,
> To thee 't is one, —

Thou art at rest, no more oppressed,
  Thy work, thy duty done.
Thou hast no more to fear, —
  The busy brain is still,
  Quiet the pulse's thrill ;
No more to hope or to regret
  Of good — or ill.

Tempests may rage above thee,
  Thou wilt not stir ;
Beyond the range of chance and change,
  Eternal voyager.
Death's gate swung open wide
  Hath let thee through
  Into the awful new, —
Into the life beyond our life,
  Of vaster view.

Over thy grave, unheeded,
  The seasons run ;
But silence and noise, passions and joys,
  Laughter and tears, are one ;
Heedless of all that is passing
  Among the loved ones here
  Once to thy heart so dear, —
Nothing of all that may here befall
  Shall reach thy ear.

Nothing ?   Ah, who shall affirm it ?
  Ah, can it be
That all we know in this world below
  Can die in the memory ?
That naught of the past shall live,
    Of the love, and the joy, and the dear
    Affections that bound us here ?
Ah, no ! if we live, they as well will live
  In another sphere.

The body we loved shall moulder
  And pass away ;
No trace or sign of the life that was
    thine
  In its earthly form shall stay.
But the spirit, — oh, where is *that ?*
    Gone, like a spoken word,
    Passed, like a vanished chord, —
Where ?   To that question, what answer
  Was ever heard ?

Here in thy grave we lay thee,
  Knowing at least
That the evil and strife of earthly life
  For thee hath ceased.
And of the life that is coming,
    The untried, vaster scope,
    Weeping here, let us hope

That we shall again be united
When the dark gates ope.

And here, by the way, I see, lying be-
side these lines, another set of verses on
somewhat the same line of thought.
Shall I read them ?
She. Do.
He.
When this frail life is over, you say,
And we from this earth have passed away,
Where stumbling we walk, with our far-
    thing light
Striving to pierce through the infinite,
Guessing and groping with Hope and
    Faith
Till the curtain dark is drawn by Death, —
Ah ! then all things which are dark to us
    here
In that Life beyond will be all made
    clear.
Then, we shall *know*.
             Perhaps —
                 Perhaps ? —
Yes, perhaps we shall know ; and then,
    perhaps,
We shall know nothing and silently lapse
Into an utter nonentity,

When naught we shall know or feel or
    see,
And nothing shall even seek to know,
Content in a negative state to be
From all Life's painful positives free
In that peace and rest that we here below
Seek for, and find not, and long for in
    vain,
Doomed through this life to struggle
    and strain,
With a glimmer of joy and hope and light
That with feeble flashes illumines our
    night.

What do you hope for with Faith so fond
In that infinite unknown life beyond,
Better than peace and an infinite rest ?
Of all that you hope, is not that the best ?

Is there anything better in life than
    sleep ?
And if Death be a long, eternal, deep
And dreamless slumber,— no care or task,
What better and sweeter could mortal
    ask ?

Ah, yes, — perhaps, — and yet, my friend,
How futile this life, if such be the end !

She. Ah, what do we know about it? Let us hope and believe, for what should we do in our sorrow without such a hope and belief? That is about the only consolation that is given to us.

He. All speculations as to what may come hereafter, when this life is over, are of course vague and dim, with no certainty, and only such expectations as Faith and Hope may give us. We cannot explain what comes after this life more than what went before it. What were we, and where were we, before we came into this world? But it is a singular fact that we never speculate as to a previous life, and only think of that in the future, which is to come after death has taken us from this. But, seek as we will, the door is shut; all that we know is that we are here now, — where we were, and where we are going, who knows? "Que scais-je?" as old Montaigne's motto reads.

She. Well, is there any use in speculating about it? The infinite "may be" must content us. With all these vast questions I do not trouble myself. I am here, and that is enough. Whatever is, is right, and whatever will be, will be, and be right. The Lord's prayer is, "Give us each day our *daily* bread," — not give us to-day to-morrow's bread. To-morrow must take care of itself, and will, doubtless. We cannot do anything to alter what is called Destiny. But we do know what our duty is, and *that* presses on us as the day goes, and generally we know what it is, — though at times we make great mistakes, and at other times willfully disobey the duties we know. But don't let us go on with these speculations as to the Future or the Past. Neither of us knows anything about them, and I don't want to have my mind disturbed by any such thoughts. Let us rather enjoy what we have. I don't think it was quite fair in you to introduce any such topics. The day is beautiful. Let us enjoy it.

He. Yes. That would be best. But as I was turning over these leaves, my eye chanced upon some verses touching on some of these questions.

She. Oh, if you have written a poem in this vein, do let me hear it ! That is a different thing from prosaic specula-

tion on what we do not know or understand. One has a right to dream, however wild one's dreams may be.

He. Now I look at these verses, they
don't seem to throw any light on what we
were saying.

She. No matter ! read them.

He. Well, such as they are, here
they are. They have only relation to
the life to come after death, not to the
life behind, before birth. They were
written after the death of a dearly
valued friend : —

Smiling if I the days recall
    When Life was glad, and Hope un-
        shaken,
Even while I smile a tear will fall
    For all that ruthless Death has taken.

And what to thee, in vain I ask,
    Hath Death, the dark, the silent, given ?
An infinite sleep, or some grand task,
    Peace — Rest — or all our hopes call
        heaven ?

I only know what was is gone
    Beyond all earthly sense and seeing, —

The smile, the form, the touch, the tone,
Have but a dim remembered being.

I only know no answers come
To all my longing, praying, sighing,
That all beyond is deaf, still, dumb,
And yields to me no faint replying.

Still I have Faith, — for what were Life,
If Faith and Hope were taken from
us ?
If after this world's strain, toil, strife,
Death should to silent nothing doom
us ?

There, — somewhere, — when this Life is
o'er,
All that seems dark here shall be
righted,
And with the loved ones gone before
We shall again be reunited.

Better that higher Hope, Faith, Trust,
Vague though it be, — howe'er un-
certain, —
Than to believe Life is but dust
When Death across it draws its cur-
tain.

She. Yes, yes ! — a hundred times yes ! For without such faith and trust we should be like sailless and rudderless ships, drifting in the dark night in a wide sea of doubt. But we do believe, we cannot help believing, say what we will.

He. Yes, let us hope, and have faith. But hope is such an *Ignis Fatuus*, and leads us so wildly astray at times.

She. I care not if it does. It is delightful even to hope for the impossible, and we are never weary of a certain kind of belief that by some miracle even our wildest hope may be realized. Reason has nothing to do with this dim condition of the mind. Though we know we are perfectly foolish in allowing some hopes to come in, still we cannot entirely drive them away. We argue with them ; thrust them out ; shut the door on them, bar it, bolt it ; fancy we have done with it ; and then in a moment it stands smiling at us, just as enticing as ever. Hope comes from the land of dreams, invents Arabian Nights, brings genii and spirits with it to transform all the world, and though Reason laughs at all these genii and phantasms of the imagination, there is always a vague somewhat which does cling to us despite our will. We take auguries from all sorts of things and events ; we believe in presentiments ; we cut for fates in books ; we woo luck ; we wish, when we first see the new moon ; we are enchanted if we find a four-leaved clover ; we think it brings luck to pick up a crooked old nail or horseshoe that lies in our path ; we wear lucky sixpences, and amulets of fortune. We know perfectly well that this is all folly, but still we have a sort of half faith in all these superstitions, don't we ?

He. Of course we do. Hope always stands on tiptoe listening and longing, and the worst or the best of it is that our foolishest hopes sometimes are realized in the most unexpected way. Are there any such things as what we call accidents ? Is not everything ruled by law ? But what the absolute law is we do not know, we only guess. Our fears, too, have quite as many superstitions as our hopes. We are afraid, some of us, to put on our left stocking first. Who dares to invite thirteen persons to table ? I have known serious persons who took particular pains to put their right foot foremost in coming into the room, lest it should bring ill-luck if they entered with the left foot first.   We think it will bring bad luck if we see the new moon over the left shoulder, or accidentally put three lights on a table.   More or less, I suspect that everybody has some pet superstition, unwilling as he may be to own it.   I admit that I have some, but I shall not tell you what they are; and you have too, have n't you?

She. Don't ask me !   Don't you think I am superior to all that foolishness ?

He. No, honestly I don't.

She. Well, I am not going to be put under cross-examination on this subject.

He. But would you dare to set out on a journey on Friday, or to be married on that day ?

She. I don't intend to be married at all, if you please.

He. But perhaps I don't please.   What will you do then ?

She. I will be married on Friday, and set off on my wedding tour the same day.

He. No, you won't, and you know you won't.   Nothing would induce you to be so foolish. What ! in despite of the Italian saying —

She. What is the Italian saying ?

He. "Ne di Venerdi, ne di Marte, non si sposa e non si parte," — not only on Friday, but on Tuesday also, you must neither set out on a journey nor be married. I confess that I should not like to begin anything on a Friday. I know this is all nonsense, and I endeavored one day to prove it to be nonsense. So a friend of mine began, with considerable self-assertion, a statue on a Friday, to show his total disbelief in such an idle superstition. He was particularly pompous in doing this. He made all his preparations on Friday, ordered all his irons to support the statue and began his statue on Friday. But, unfortunately for the experiment, after a fortnight of hard work, during which all went wrong, to his great mortification he was finally obliged to pull it all down and begin anew.

She. And everybody laughed at him, and said : " I told you so."

He. Of course they did.

She. And was he obstinate, and did he

renew his experiment and begin again on a Friday ?

He. No ; he did not. He had had enough of it. He bowed down humbly and courted Fortune in despite of his principles, and began anew on Monday, it being agreed that Monday is a lucky day, and all went well. I must tell you too another experience of mine, in which I owed my life to my obeying the superstition against setting out on a journey on Friday. That was the day when it was far more convenient for me to go than any other. I was pressed for time, all my preparations were made, when I said to myself : "What's the use, better have all the luck one can get. It is all very foolish, but — but I will wait till to-morrow." And lucky it was that I did, for the very train in which I should have been, had I left on Friday, had a terrible accident, and I know not how many passengers were killed and maimed and ruined for life. What do you say to that ?

She. Oh, what a lucky superstition it was ! If I had such experiences I should not dare to do anything on Friday.

He. But apropos to what we were saying a few moments ago about our hopes and fears, I think I have two little poems here somewhere, touching upon this subject. Ah, yes ; here they are. I will read them to you.

She. Do.

He. First I will read you this, which is only a fear, — one of those fears which come over us at the very height of our happiness ; one of those dark thoughts which suddenly shadow the spirit with terror, and make us feel that nothing in life, even at its culmination of joy and love, is secure.

My dearest heart, my life, my joy, my
    love,
  Even as I gaze into thy loving eyes,
And feel their blessing like the heavens
    above,
  At times the o'erwhelming thought and
    fear will rise
Lest thou be taken from me, and, be-
    reft
  Of thy dear presence, life's sad rem-
    nant through

I with dead memories, graves of joy, be
  left.
  Ah, then what should I do ? What
    should I do ?

Pray God that this may never, never be.
  And yet, how vain the hope ! Too
    well I know
That hour must come at last to you, — to
  me ;
  We cannot both together hope to go.
Death will not take us both into its
  arms,
  And bear us both together to its rest,
Else death would be all free from life's
  alarms,
  And be as to a child its mother's
    breast.

But ah ! the fearful thought, like some
  dark cloud,
  Comes o'er my spirit, that at last,
    alone,
I may be left, with spirit sad and bowed,
  Joyless to tread life's mournful jour-
    ney on.
Oh, my dear love, stay with me to the
  end !

My hope, my joy, my life, oh, stay
   with me !
Till the dark gates of death shall open,
   lend
The blessing of thy love, — my angel
   be.

She. That last hope is too selfish.
Ah, to go together is the true wish of
love, — that neither should be left to tread
life's dreary remnant alone after the
other is taken. And yet how vain to
wish, how useless to hope, that any such
consummation of life can ever take
place !

He. Yes ; but what is horrible in an-
ticipation, what is equally terrible in fact
when it comes, we have to bear, and
Time, the only assuager of sorrow, finally
throws a veil over our deepest griefs.

She. Yes ; but life is never the same
afterwards. It has for all of us a different aspect, a different sentiment. The
best of its melodies are played in a
lower and a minor tone. The glad lift,
the impassioned utterance, the bounding
hope, the unquestioning joy and faith,
the confidence in life, are ours no more.

We have to learn the sadder lesson of
patience. We hold life's flowers in our
hand with a looser grasp, and almost
expect them to fall, thankful if they are
ours for a moment.

He. Yes ; life is only a black-letter
text : —

Not till the light of joy has passed away,
   The orb of patience rises full and
      great
To rule our life with soft and shadowy
      sway,
   And sanctify the ruins wrought by
      fate.

When sorrow calls us, from the feast we
      rise ;
   Its lights are glaring, trivial are its
      smiles,
And Thought walks on through buried
      memories
   Like some cowled monk along the
      tomb-strewn aisles.

We wend to silence. In its cell we sit
   And read the mournful missal of man's
      fate,

The sad black-letter text in which is writ
  E'en the illumined chapter of the
  great.

Girt round by walls we never can o'er-
  peer,
  With one dark gate where all our
  pathways end,
Puzzled we stand, in hope and yet in fear,
  Unknowing where the ceaseless passers
  wend.

"Farewell," they say. "To love and
  joy we go."
  We have not faith, or we should smile
  again.
But ah, we beat the gate, and, wild with
  woe,
  We struggle like a madman with his
  chain.

Yet with this farthing candle of our faith
  Into the dark, dread, vast beyond we
  peer,
Where each beholds upon the blank of
  death
  The trembling shadows of his hope or
  fear.

She. Don't let us go into these dark questions, to which we none of us can find any sufficient answer except in our hope and our faith.

He. But do what we will, we cannot help asking these questions and longing vainly for some definite answer. Unless, indeed, we accept the "we are told," and calmly, without taking the trouble even to think (which is, perhaps, of not much use after all), lay our heads down on the steps of the Church and take for granted all that it says.

She. Oh, I am not going to allow myself to be drawn into any religious discussions. I did not come out here into the woods for that.

He. And I am afraid if we did we should find ourselves at last entirely in the woods, and utterly lost, not in the least knowing the way out or on. So let us stay where we are. But now that we are in this mood, let me read you a poem which is somewhat in the same tone of thought, and ought to go with the other.

She. Do.

He.

You pray to God, now as a power of love
  Who will forgive you all the sins you
    tell ;
Now as a stern, unpardoning power
    above,
  To all those sins and faults implacable.

You make Him share dominion over all
  With the dark tempter, unto whom is
    given
The strength to thwart his every plan,
    and call
  The soul to hell which He had framed
    for heaven.

I envy you your faith, your fixed belief
  That you the secret of the soul pos-
    sess,
Sure of its future when this life, so brief,
  Hath passed away to utter nothingness.

All that I know is that I nothing know ;
  All is a vague and clouded mystery.
Whence we have come, and whither we
    shall go,
  And why we all are here is dark to
    me.

God hath created man, you say.   To me
  Rather it seems, when the wide world
    I scan,
With all the myths and dreams of his-
    tory,
  Man hath created God, and not God
    man ;

Created God after the image crude
  Of his own being, like some tyrant
    king,
Whose purpose prayer can change ; who
    must be wooed
  By self-abasement, pain, and suffering.

If we are good, our spirits are not stirred
  By love of justice, honor, virtue, love,
But for the sake of some vague, dim re-
    ward
  That may be given in some life above.

She. I am afraid there is something
only too true in that last thought, for
surely if we look through history we
find that man has always shaped his God
after his own individuality, and given
Him at all periods of time the shape,
form, and characteristic spirit, as well as
features, of a human being.

He. And now, if you are not too much
bored, I should like to read you another
copy of verses, as our grandfathers used
to call them, before we quit this subject and train of thought. Perhaps it is
a little too gloomy and serious for a summer's morning like this, but if you are
to hear it at all, you may be, after the
last poem, somewhat in its vein, and
might like to hear it now.

She. Pray read it.

He.

I stand in the midnight silence,
    The throbbing stars are above me,
And alone I stand, and I long for the
        lost
Who used to cherish and love me.
To the infinite distance beyond
    I stretch out my hands imploring :
Oh, give me one word, — one word, I
        cry,
    All my soul in my prayer outpouring.

With an infinite longing, a prayer
    That is wordless, I cry, — with a yearn-
        ing,
A hope beyond hope, all my soul going
        forth ;

And then, with no answer returning; —
In its passion my spirit uplifts
   Like a wave on its high crest swaying,
All shattered to fall, with a baffled
     sense
   Of the vanity of all praying.

No answer, no sign, no answer ;
   Blank silence to all this craving.
All nature, all heaven, — deaf, dumb to
     us, —
   All our longing mere empty raving.
God by no sign declaring
   He listens to pity or love us,
But, leaving us here in our ignorant
     blindness,
   Outstretches no hand above us.

How many hearts are breaking,
   How many weeping and sighing,
How many darkly despairing,
   How many starving and dying ;
How many praying and praying,
   With wildest imploring ; but never
Comes back the least answering word or
     sign,
   And Death's secret is kept forever.

The mystery who can unriddle
By which we are ever haunted ?
To Life's terrible question — Death's in-
finite puzzle —
What answer was ever granted ?
Wherever we go it pursues us,
When we seek to grasp it it flies us,
And despite all our longings, our ques-
tions, our prayers,
The secret forever defies us.

All Nature is unrelenting,
Tears and prayers are alike unavailing
To touch her pity. Cold, cruel, and
hard,
She heeds not our pain or our ailing.
To the good, to the bad, as by chance,
Fates gives both her stripes and ca-
resses ;
Do all that we can, what avails it at
last ?
As she chooses, she curses or blesses.

Where, then, shall we turn in our grief
When life's burdens upon us are
lying ?
When despair at the heart's door is
knocking,

And to prayer there is no replying ?
Ah, well !   What we know is nothing,
  What we hope for, almost beyond
    hoping ;
But still let us hope, and let faith be our
    staff
While here we are blindly groping.

We have but to bow our heads,
  And humbly accept what is given.
The veil of the future no mortal can lift,
  Nor show us a glimpse of it even.
Life to come is a guess, at the best,
  At a vague perfection of beauty.
But the life we have here is ours, and we
    know
  That its law should be love and duty.

She. Yes, that is sad enough, and true
enough.   What do we really know about
anything ?   But still one must have faith
in something and hope for something,
though it passes all understanding.   All
nature is deaf to our longing and dumb
to our asking, as much in our griefs as in
our joys.   It never really sympathizes
with us, except, perhaps, in our calmest
moods.   To our passions and longings and
cravings, it has no answering voice.

He. Ay ; and not only to our deep emotions of passion or sorrow it does not respond, but often seems to stand before us calm, silent, with a tantalizing smile, almost of scorn, or to answer to our appeals with a discordant tone that jars on all our sensibilities. For instance, —

'Neath the tree where we first told our
     love
Despairing I stand, all alone,
All alone in this dear, happy grove,
    And weep for the days that are flown.
Crying out in my bitterest grief,
Is there no one to give me relief
And help me this sorrow to bear ?
    And I know there is no one, — not one ;
There is nothing but Nature, and what
     does she care
    For the past and the lost and the gone ?
What help can she give ? All the sky,
     all the air,
Is as gleamingly happy, as cloudlessly
     fair,
    As if pain, death, and grief were unknown.
No sorrow, no sadness is hers !
Through the leaves up the hillside a soft
     whisper stirs,

The banks with gay wild-flowers are
    strewn ;
The birds are all singing their fresh
    matin song,
And the brook babbling gayly goes purl-
    ing along
    To gladden each pebble and stone.
All is sunshine and springtime, all Nature
    rejoices,
No voice but of gladness I hear in her
    voices,
    Not a note, not a tone
Of sorrow or sadness, — but all things
    cry out
In their freshness and joy with a jubilant
    shout, —
    And I so alone,
So wretched that all I can think of is
    death
    And the days that are flown.

Oh, Nature, so silent, so heartless, so
    cruel,
    Have you nothing to me to say ?
I know but too well there is no more re-
    newal
    For all that has passed away.
    But why be so glad and so gay,

As if all of this life was pure joy,
  With sorrow and death coming never
  The fondest and dearest to sever,
Unrelenting to blast and destroy ?
Why torture my heart with your glad-
    ness,
  Why sing with such careless delight,
While my soul, in the depths of its sad-
    ness,
  Is dark with the darkness of night ? —
Of a night when not even a star
  Can be seen to illume
In the heavens so clouded, so far,
  Its hopeless and terrible gloom.

If you cannot console me, oh, help me to
    bear,
  At least, what I cannot forget.
Weep with me, storm with me, come to
    me and share
  Life's darkness and grief and re-
    gret ;
Tell over with me all the memories dear,
  All the joys that are lost, that are
    past ;
Oh, be not so cold, irresponsively fair,
  Lay your hand on my breast, give me
    rest, give me rest ;

Cloud the skies, all too bright in their joy
    and their light,
And with tears all the world overcast.

She. I am afraid we have got into too
sad a vein. The day is too bright for
such strains, for it is somewhat like what
you have described in this poem. And I
am happy to say that I see no thunder
cloud rising yet, though it may come upon
us, and will be sure to if you write a
poem about it. See if you can't find some
poem in which you take a little more
happy view of life. I think we have
been sad long enough. I should like to
hear something more paradisiacal now.
Can't you transport me into some ideal
spot, where there is nothing to weep over
and mourn over or regret?

He. I am afraid all these latter verses
are wearisomely sad. I will look and
see if I cannot find something a little
less gloomy. Ah, yes! here is one that
perhaps you will find as much too ideal
as the others were too sadly real. At all
events, it will serve for a change, for another kind of movement after all these
largos and adagios.

Smile, dearest, smile !
   Thy love to me
Is life's enchanted isle
   In its deep sea.

Stately and tall,
   There grows the palm ;
There peace broods over all,
   Beauty and calm.

Whispers the wind,
   Murmurs the sea ;
All is so sweet and kind,
   There I would be.

Blue are the skies,
   Fathomless, deep,
Softly the clouds that rise
   Over them sweep.

All there is bloom,
   Tenderness, grace,
Never the thought of doom
   Haunts that blest place.

No storms' wild rage,
   No toil, no strife ;
There is the golden age,
   There love and life.

Worn out with care,
Weary, oppressed,
Let me seek solace there,
Let me find rest.

She. Well, that is an ideal land, such as we never see ; however, we long for it.

He. Oh, yes.   Love finds it easily.

She. If you say so, of course it is so, for I suppose you know. But, unfortunately, I am very ignorant of those southern seas and enchanted isles.

He. I do not profess to know anything about it, but I guess, I fancy, I imagine there must be some such Elysium, — at least in dreams there is, and why not in reality, — where the breeze is ever mild and the air ever perfumed ; where the flowers grow without attendance or care ; where even the rain sings as it falls ; where nothing is harsh, and all things are perfect, as they are in the Elysian fields.

She. Perhaps it was in the garden where Adam first met Eve, and she gave him that fatal apple. I suppose it must have been a place into which the devil never entered, or at least before he entered ; afterwards, you know, there was

a terrible shindy. Cain got terribly
angry about something, I don't know precisely what.

He. Yes ; I think I have heard of it,
and that our progenitor found consolation
in a woman of Nod. Where Nod is,
and where the woman came from, and how
she happened to be there, and who made
her, are questions I cannot answer, but I
have always felt the greatest interest in
it and her. The nearest approximation I
have ever made to the land of Nod is a
dreamland, and perhaps the woman
there too was a dream. At all events, I
cannot help desiring to know a little
more about her, if only because she was
our earliest ancestress.

She. Then she must have been beautiful, as we have already agreed.

He. You know it was awkward for
Cain to have nobody to marry, — not even
a sister.

She. Yes, rather, I suppose. But who
was this woman of Nod ? I believe you
invented her.

He. On the contrary, she invented me.
As for who she was, I refer you to Gen-
esis.

She. I shall read it carefully.

He. And I hope you will understand it. As for the first chapters, about the generations of men, I confess I do not, and I see no light as to who our original ancestress was, whether we came from Seth, or from Cain and the woman of Nod, and whether Eve's name was not Adam.

She. What do you mean?

He. Why, you remember that in one account of creation there, God created them male and female, and called *them* Adam, don't you? And in that last account there does not seem to have been any Cain or any Abel, unless Cainan, the grandson of Seth, was he.

She. Don't ask me what I remember, for I remember nothing about any of them except what everybody knows about Adam and Eve and Cain and Abel, and I don't wish to talk about them, or think about them here.

He. Well, you remember Paradise at least, and how charming it was until that event of the apple. With your permission, I am going to take you there, just for a moment.

She. Do, I beg you.

He.

'T was in the lovely month of May ;
  Clear was the heaven's azure tent,
Save where some cloudlet, lost, astray,
  Loitering along its blue field went ;
The world was sown with flowers ; the
    breeze,
All perfumed, stirred the blossoming
    trees ;
And o'er the green path through the wood
A tender spirit seemed to brood,
As we two wandered, idly, slow,
  With throbbing hearts, not quite at
    ease, —
Ah, dearest ! yes, you know, — you
    know, —
'T was not so very long ago, —
  Beneath these silent, shadowy trees.

More than we had what cared we for ?
  We loved, and did not that suffice
A light on everything to pour
  As pure as that of Paradise ?
The world was fresh with youth and
    spring ;
What had the orioles then to sing
We did not know as well as they,
And better, too ! — for it was May,

And we were young, and scarcely knew
  A wish beyond the passing hour,
And both our hearts were opening too,
And glowing with love's tender hue,
  Like any opening flower.

And there it was our love we told,
  With many an inner hope and doubt,
But once 't was said, we grew more bold,
  And love put all our fears to rout.
Birds sang ; the woods their light leaves
      shook,
With glad, gay voice laughed out the
      brook,
And all the world around, above,
Cried out to us : Love, only love.
Ah, dearest ! yes, you know they did ;
  No voice of nature there
Our happy troth of love forbid,
Our happy utterances chid,
  All seemed its bliss to share.

  There ; there is no mourning in that, is
there ?

  She. It is charming ; and I hope all
this happiness lasted, for when he uttered
what he did, you know, he was still under
the spell and the charm.   The mourn-

ing, I suppose, came in much later, if it
came at all, as I hope it did not. For
my own part, I am happy to leave them
where they are. I do not wish to forecast the possibilities of the future. I
confess I was afraid that some sadness
would come in at the end.

He. Sadness always comes in at the
end of everything. Life at such heights
does not last. But I think we can leave
them there to wander in their Elysium without forecasting or intruding.
Whether that day, bright and clear as it
was, ended in a thunderstorm, or, worse,
in a gray mist, I know not, and care not.
Nor do I care whether Cain killed Abel the
next day, and I am perfectly willing to
say that if he did, he probably knew why
he did, though I don't. Perhaps it had
something to do with the woman of Nod.

She. Oh, don't let us talk any more
about any of those people, but rather
read me something else. You see that I
am like the daughter of the Horse-leech,
who always said, Give ! give ! When I
looked into that mysterious book of yours
you showed me, I saw something there
about hopes and fears. If it is not too
sad, will you read it to me ?

He. I am afraid it is not very gay, but, such as it is, here it is at your service. At all events, it has more to do with hopes than with fears, if I remember it right.

She. If you remember it right? I like that. You know that you remember every word of it.

He. I know nothing of the kind. You don't suppose I burthen my memory with all the rubbish I write. Gott bewahr! or, as my English friend translated it, God beware! I have something better to do, I hope, than that; nor do I believe I could repeat by memory a single poem of all that I have written. The fact is that I thrust them away, and try to forget all about them, so that when I look over them I possibly may put myself in the position of a third person, and exercise a little of my judgment upon them. I scribble them on all sorts of fragments of paper, too. That is a fad of mine. A great white, spotless sheet almost frightens me. It seems like a sort of challenge. But with any old, worthless sheet I feel more at ease, more familiar, more, as it were, in my dressing-

gown. I don't think I could sit down
in a dress coat and white choker, and
take out a clean, beautiful, hot-pressed
sheet of paper and write what you call
a poem on it, of malice prepense, as it
were.

She. Well, but the poem.

He. Here it is.

'T is the postman's knock I hear.
    What has he come to bring ?
Hope looks out of my heart, and fear
    Of nothing — of everything.
A foolish hope of I know not what ;
An idle fear of nothing begot,
    That still in my heart will spring
    With an anxious questioning.

Every hour at my heart
    Knocks a fear and a hope, —
Half glad, half sad ; at the summons I
        start,
    And the door to hope's promise ope, —
And there Disappointment sneering
        stands,
Only to show me his empty hands
    With his cheating horoscope,
    And no star in the heaven's whole cope.

Yet under all fears will spring
  A hope that I cannot quell,
That the very next knock may bring
  The surprise of a miracle.
Some Ginn from the world of dreams to
      say :
" Order, great master, your slave will
    obey.
  There is nothing impossible,
  As we spirits know full well."

And then I shall answer, — oh, what,
  What shall I answer ?   Who knows ?
Make the whole world for me what it is
      not,
  Make it a world of rose ;
Make it what dreamers have dreamt it
    might be,
When life and love are in sympathy,
  And beauty forever flows,
  And hope to reality grows.

Make it both young and old ;
  Make it both gentle and strong ;
Sweep away care to the devil's fold,
  Purge all this life from wrong.
Lift me, set joy on the mountains,
Till life from its myriad fountains

Fill all the earth with its song,
While the angels its chorus prolong.

Not from one only, — from all
   Lift the great burden of life ;
Strip from the weary world its pall
   Of sorrow and pain and strife ;
Spread the broad banner of peace,
Bid all life's cruelty cease
   That now in the world is rife,
   And strikes at the heart like a knife.

Dream of wild dreams, not to be,—
   Not to be here, at least.
Ah, hope's mirage !   Shall we see
   Thy perfection when life has ceased ?
Will the promise so dear, so ideal,
In the world of the future be real,
   When the soul from this world is re-
      leased,
   And humanity's hunger appeased ?

Perhaps, though I see not how,
   For the knocking of doubt and fear,
Beating forever, dull and low,
   At the door of my heart I hear.
Is it the knock of some mighty Ginn,
Or an angel's or devil's now coming in ?

An angel to wipe away every tear,
Or a fiend, with his old habitual sneer,
  To tempt us to death and sin ?

She. I don't think you quite knew
what you wanted. But no matter. If
we are to have a visit from the other
world, pray let us have a Ginn. I have
a longing to see a Ginn, for I was
brought up on "The Arabian Nights,"
and I know they can do anything they
please.

He. You mean "The Arabian Nights"
as we read it in the old English version ;
but, I am sorry to say, in the original it
certainly was not written for delicate
ears. There has been a translation of
this of late years into English, but I
recommend you not to look into it, —
Burton's, — but if you see the cover of it,
let that suffice. Guardi e passi.

She. Are we ever visited by spirits of
any kind — good or evil — from the unknown world of mystery ? My notion is
that they are born of ourselves, and are
only haunting ghosts of our desires,
exhalations rising up with or without
our call, like those that came from the

Fisherman's jar, and assuming form before us.

He. I am really very sorry, but I cannot answer that question satisfactorily, because I never saw a spirit. Stop! when I say I never saw a spirit, I mean with my bodily eyes and when I was awake. In my dreams I have seen many a one, and the other night I had a long visit from a Ginn, or something that said it was a Ginn ; and, for all I know, it was one.

She. And what did he say ?

He. I am afraid he was a very tempting spirit. However, you must decide. I will read to you a little record made the next morning of the chief things he said to me. No ; on the whole, I won't read it now. I see that it is long, and, I am afraid, rather prosy, and does not quite do justice to my Ginn. I will read it some other time.

She. Some other time never comes. We are told, " Seize the present by the forelock," whatever that may be.

He. " Seize *Time*," is it not ? Poor old fellow, he is bald enough behind, but according to all the representations of him by painters and poets, he has one lock left on his forehead, and that is what we are requested to seize ; why, I don't know.

She. Yes, you do ; it is to stop him, and enable you to break his hour-glass.

He. So it is.

She. But about the Ginn. I prefer him to old Father Time.

He. No, not to-day, to-morrow. Sitting too long at any banqueting-table, although you are provided with the most exquisite of viands and the most delicious of wines (as of course you have been to-day), is sure to produce an indigestion. You've had enough for to-day, and more than enough, and so have I. Let us go and wander about through these delightful woods. I can show you the haunts of fairies under the cool, green shadows, and pure, deep wells where the Naiads bathe, and groves where the Dryads nestle, and beds of wild-flowers on which Titania might sleep. These woods are full of wonders to any one who has the eye to see them.

She. Yes, to any one who has the eye to see them and the soul to appreciate them. Nature to man is what he is. We only find what we bring. The seeing is in the spirit, not the eye, and all things take the shape and color of the mind.

He. I have a little poem, in which I have endeavored to embody that idea, and I will read it to you some day, if you like.

She. Read it now.

He. I have n't it here.

She. Well, will you bring it to-morrow and read it, — and the Ginn?

He. Yes.

She. You promise?

He. I promise.

She. Well, in that case, we will make a pause for to-day, and perhaps it will be better so. And to-morrow, at the same hour and the same place, we will meet again, and you will bring some more poems. Will you not? And one word more: you must forgive me for all my apparent flippancy in what I have said, and for my foolish comments and criticisms. Believe me, my dear friend, your poems have often touched me deeply, and I cannot fitly thank you for your kindness in reading them to me. In fact, I cannot tell you how deeply they have touched me, and all my flippancy is but a veil thrown often over myself to conceal what I scarcely dared to own. Put it down to my shyness and inability to express myself, won't you? Pray do. There are times when we cannot, we dare not, give expression to what moves us within, and we strive to throw off our feelings by a laugh or a banter when tears are too near, and we dare not give way to our impulses. You will make all excuses for me, won't you?

He. You do not need them, I assure you. I think we know each other and can trust each other.

She. And you will bring me some more poems and read them to me to-morrow?

He. Certainly I will, if you really wish it. But we have had enough for to-day, and now let us drop the curtain and enjoy the entr'acte by wandering through the woods and breathing this pure, delightful air. And I will order Monsieur Cobweb to get his weapons in his hand, and kill you a red-hipped humble-bee on the top of a thistle, and bring you the honey bag. Will that satisfy you?

She. Yes, provided you also bring Peasblossom and Mustard Seed and sweet Bully Bottom and his company. Then, indeed, it will be "a most courageous day — a most happy hour!"

[So finished that day's reading. The next morning, at the same hour and in the same place, they met, according to agreement. It does not do for me, for I am only an intruder, a chiel taking notes, to say how pretty she looked, — lovely, I ought to say, — and how sweetly she smiled as she greeted him. She began the conversation.]

She. Well, you are as good as your word. Here you are, as you promised to be, and with more poems, I hope.

He. Did not you know I should be?

She. H'm, h'm! I hoped — I did not quite trust — poets are very slippery fellows.

He. How did you suppose I could break such a promise? In the first place, you were to be here, and in the next place, you had spread the glamour of your flattery over me by asking me to read more

verses to you.   Did any poet or poet-
aster ever refuse such inducements and
turn his back to such an invitation ?

She. And now that all the proper preliminary flourishes have been made, suppose we begin.   Let it be conceded that
I am the most beautiful of beings, the
most flattering of women, and you are
the perfectest of poets.

He. I never said either the one thing or
the other.

She. Then you do not admit that I am
the most beautiful of beings ?

He. I only objected that I did not say
so.   Whatever I may think, I did not
put those thoughts into words.   Of
course I know that I am the perfectest
of poets, and that nothing ever was so
faultless in thought and form and expression as these verses of mine, and that
the world is utterly foolish and miserably
mean not to acknowledge this.   But
somehow or other, mortifying as it is,
the world has not as yet recognized
their wonderful charm.   Posterity, of
course, will, but I don't know that I shall
be any better for that.

She. You should take a return ticket,

and come back unexpectedly and see.
Wreaths and laurels are, for the most
part, laid by the world upon the grave,
not upon the living head.

He. Oh, I think, on the whole, we get
what we deserve in this world while we
are living. Nay, perhaps I should say
at times a good deal more, but at all
events an ample and hearty recognition
of our merits as authors. For instance,
I took up a little book this morning,
and in the fly leaves at the end I found a
series of extracts from numerous notices
of some recent American books in vari-
ous American papers, and I confess I
was as much surprised as delighted on
reading them. I knew that some of the
American writers were very clever and
amusing, but I confess that I had no idea
that some of the writers of novelettes and
short stories possessed such an amazing
power and genius. I find in three pages
of notices, given to three authors, that
one — a lady, of course — "has imagination, breadth, and a daring and courage
oftenest spoken of as masculine;" more-
over, that she is "exquisitely ideal, and
her ideals are of an exalted order;" that

she "has made a conquest so complete
and astonishing as at once to give her
fame;" that she has "wealth of imagination and exuberance of striking
language," "straightforward grace that
captures the sympathy of the reader,"
"freshness of feeling and a mingling of
pathos and humor which are *simply delicious.*" I find also that the next author
whose works are noticed "may easily
become the novelist-laureate" (whatever that may be); that "she strikes a
new and richly loaded vein;" that she
"has a wealth of womanly love and tenderness." The third author noticed has
"a portfolio of *delightsome* studies,"
"musings on a golden granary full to the
brim," "true insight, polished irony, a
light and indescribable touch which lifts
you over a whole sea of froth and foam"
"to the true heart and soul of the
theme;" one of his books is pronounced
a "noble volume," with "rare fascina-
tion of style and thought," "delicacy of
discrimination and appreciation," "con-
summate art;" it "reports perfectly and
with exquisite humor all the *fugacious*
and manifold emotions," and is, in a

word, "bewitching." All this may be
very true. I do not deny it, for I have
never read these astonishing works. All
I have to say is that no greater praise,
nor more peculiar expressions of it, can
be given to the — as yet supposed to be
— greatest of English writers. I think
at least that the authors of these works
must be satisfied, and perhaps blush at
these extraordinary eulogiums, if authors
can blush. But at all events, they cannot complain that they have not received
while living an enthusiastic recognition
of the great merit of their works.
What will happen after they are dead,
who knows ? Death has something sa-
cred in it, and often begets exaggeration
of the merits of those who are gone.
I am generally surprised to find, as I
always do in all obituaries, what a wonderful genius, what an able statesman,
what a "supreme" poet (that, I believe,
is the correct epithet), X was. He
seemed to me to be rather a commonplace man until he died.

She. Yes, death sanctifies everything.
Seen through that veil, even the harshest
facts of life have a softer and kindlier

aspect, and are subdued into tenderer light.   But the honors and praises of the world come but too often too late, when the spirit they would have cheered is gone, when the ear that would have heard them with gratitude and delight is beyond the reach of human words. We miss so many opportunities in life to do kind actions.   We are so chary of our praise.   We are sometimes too shy to utter what lies in our hearts.   We distrust our impulses to say even kind words until it is too late.   Out of mere modesty and false shame we often refrain from giving voice to our feelings.

He. Yes, yes ; undoubtedly, as you say, the honors and praises are showered on the dead which would have cheered them living.

Too late, too late, your honors and your
     praise.
Could you not speak ere death had closed
     the ear
And stilled the heart that would have
     leaped to hear ?
What is the use that now, too late, you
     raise

The tardy monument, and fling your lays
Upon the senseless clay, that joy or fear
Or loud applause or blame or critic sneer
Can reach not where he walks beyond
  life's ways ?
While here alive and sensitive he went,
Unto his living heart your words had sent
A thrill of joy his pathway to illume ;
Now, when your praise and honors all are
  vain,
What serves it that your useless wreaths
  are lain
Upon his grave to deck his silent tomb ?

She. Ah, what serves it, indeed ! To
console, perhaps, the friends who are left
behind. But what avails it to him who is
gone ? Too late is a terribly sad lesson
and reproach.

He. As you were saying, death sanctifies, but memory enhances what we have
lost, and art embalms. The charms that
life steals gradually away have a peren-
nial youth. In memory's art they live
in perpetual youth.

She. Yes, and in perpetual regret. Can
one in age see one's portrait, painted in
youth, without a sigh ? This was what
I once was, and now ! Ah me !

He. That is the thought which I have endeavored to express in these lines :—

And this was painted from her face
  Some hundred years ago,
When she was young, glad, full of grace,
  In life's first bloom and glow.
Here June and joy unfading live,
  Here youth and springtime stay,
While she, heart-weary, worn with grief,
  Passed, years ago, away ;

Passed in the ripeness of her years,
  When she was sad, gray, old,
Oppressed with cares, depressed by fears,
  Life's young romance all told.
But here no tears are in those eyes,
  No lines are on this brow,
And age, death, sadness she defies
  In Art's eternal now.

She. We must all come to it. The thought that old age must come to us, unless death interposes, is a sad one. But there is no help for it.

He. Suppose things had been arranged in the entirely opposite way, — that it was ordained to us to be born old, and daily and yearly to grow younger and fresher and gladder, and that time, instead of constantly robbing us of our youth, should as constantly carry us back to it.

She. And where would you stop ? At the prime of manhood or womanhood ? Would not death then seem more cruel than when it comes, as now, after the grasp on life has been loosed and the glamour of youth is gone ?

He. Perhaps ; but suppose it went on further than that, to the child's life, and to the infant's life, and then to die in the arms of our mother, knowing and fearing nothing ?

She. There would not then be any living mother. She would have passed away as a child or an infant herself.

He. That is a difficulty, and perhaps, after all, it is better as it is. However, I shall have to think out this scheme, and see what arrangements I can make to obviate this difficulty, and then I will let you know.

She. Well ; I will wait in patience for the solution. But now let us go on to the Ginn, if there is any such a poem.

The Ginn! the Ginn! I say. Let me hear what the Ginn said.

He. No; wait a moment. First I must do justice to Goethe, and correct the impression I made on your mind yesterday. You may remember that I quoted two lines of his about the barking of dogs. I could only quote those two lines, for I had quite forgotten all the rest. But after returning home I looked up the passage. It occurs in what he calls an Elegy, and I think it but fair to him to say that, however he hates the barking of dogs in general, he makes a special exception in favor of a particular dog. His Elegy runs thus. Shall I read it to you in the original German, or translate it?

She. Oh, translate it, by all means.

He. All translations are poor. Even the best are like the reversed side of the tapestry, and mine is not the best, but they give, at all events, the sense and the rhythm of the verses.

Many noises are hateful to me, but, far
    above others,
The barking of dogs I hate ; yelping,
    they tear at my ears.

One dog only I know that I hear very
    often with pleasure,
Barking, baying, — the dog that to my
    neighbor belongs.
For once at my maiden he barked while
    she was quietly sitting
Here at my side, and so nearly our secret
    betrayed.
Now when I hear him bark, I think she
    is coming, is coming,
Or I remember the time when she was
    longed for — and came.

She. Well, that is some alleviation, at
least, to his general condemnation · of
dogs, and I take back my reproval, — that
is, partially, not wholly. He could not
have had any dog of his own, to say
what he did. However, a little is better
than nothing, and we lovers of dogs must
content ourselves with the crumbs that
are thrown to us, as the dogs do.

He. No ; they do not content themselves. They will not let us alone. They
leap up, and scratch at us, and sit up on
their hind legs, and beg and pray for
more, whatever you give them.

She. Poor little things ; why should n't
they ?

He. And why should they? I like dogs very well in their place. But that is not when we are at table, and eating.

She. And what is their place?

He. The place of Fritz is, I suppose, in your lap. At least, he seems to think so, and so do you, if I may judge from what I see; for he is never content unless he is there.

She. Don't let us talk any more about dogs. You and I shall never agree upon that subject, so be kind enough to let me hear what the Ginn said to you.

He. I suppose I shall have to read it now.

She. Yes, you will.

He. So be it. Here it is.

A GINN.

With a prayer to the Power above I laid
    my head on my pillow,
And into the realms of silence,
The dim, hushed world of silence, that is
    far beyond even dreaming,
The blank, vague, far-off nowhere of
    utter unconsciousness,
    My spirit was borne away.

And there, as I drifted, I know not how
long, knowing nothing,
Slowly there issued to me, out of the
silence and void,
A strange, mysterious voice, and a
strange, mysterious shape,
So dim it was scarcely a shape, so faint
it was scarcely a voice,
That cried to me, " Listen and hear."

At these words in my sleep I started,
then back again, utterly helpless,
I sank, and I drifted away into the realm
of dreams.
And the voice cried, "Fear not, fear not ;
listen, and do not fear.
I am banished from what, in your fool-
ishness, you deem heaven,
But me no power can destroy.
There cannot be good without evil,
Or what men in their blindness call
evil ;
All positives negatives need, or else they
could not exist,
And as long as God's positive lives, his
negatives also will live.
This is one half of creation ; the other
half is my master's ;
Turn to me, then, and hear.

For 't is he who has bid me to come, and
whisper to you a message.
Bend to me.   Thou shalt hear.

"I have stood and listened behind the
dim, drawn curtain of death,
And heard the secret words, and the
things that are to be.
Vainly the heavenly guards have hurled
at me, as I listened,
Their flashing arrows of fire.
With the lightning's power they came,
But I laughed at them and their threat,
For my master protected me.
Listen ! hark ! I will whisper those hid-
den secrets to thee,
So thou mayst know, and live, —
Know the things that are coming, the
secrets of joy, death, life.

"Think you by prayer to change God's
purposes, foolish mortal ? —
Prayer, and the intercession of what you
call saints and angels ?
No ! there is none who can alter or sway
his slightest intent.
Has He listened once to your prayers ?
Has He answered you ever, or given you
aught that He promised ?

Has He paid you with joy for your ser-
    vice, or scourged you to it with
    thongs,
Saying that pain is the path you must
    travel to come to Him ?

" Which is the God you worship ?   Is it
    Zeus, Jehovah, or Baal,
Isis, Osiris, Jupiter, Christus, or whom ?
Whichever it be, has He given you joy in
    this human life,
Or only promised a joy when this life on
    earth shall be past ? —
A wretched 'perhaps' of bliss for a
    present of toil, grief, pain !
Turn, then, to me ; all the joys they
    promise to you in the future
My master will give to you here."

And he bent down his head, and whis-
    pered,
    And I heard, and lost all my senses,
And convulsions and mania seized me,
And I struggled, and cried out wildly,
    As if a demon possessed me.
And what I heard I can tell not,
    For all that I heard seems a dream,
That hovers about in my brain, and is all
    beyond my reach,

And I cannot utter it.
I grasp at it with my thoughts afire, out-
stretched in the darkness,
But it flies, and evades my touch. Yet
still it is there !
There, whispering dimly, strangely ;
there, hovering out of sight ;
There, tempting with promises vague, and
wild, mysterious words,
To flee with it far away
Into boundless regions of beauty, and
glory, and grace, and gladness,
Beyond all sorrow and care,
Where knowledge of all shall be given,
And the secret of all explained,
Where power shall be granted beyond all
human seeing and knowing,
Where the wildest hope of the spirit shall
blossom in perfect flower.
When the shadow of sleep comes on, it
whispers, "Come to me, mortal,
I have the key that opens the gates of all
earthly delights.
Linger not here, but come.
I am he who whispered in time long ago
to Mohammed.
Maraka, the aged and blind, knew me,
and heard what I said,

Crying out, 'Koddus, Koddus. Verily,
    this is the Namus.'
And the Korybantes knew me, for it was
    I that possessed them ;
And the Thyades, and the Mænads, and
    the Lenæ, and Mirmillones,
As they flung their arms about, and
    shouted, and clanged their cym-
    bals ; —
And Pythia heard my voice, and her
    oracles were my whispers,
And all the Bacchantes as well, and the
    soothsayers all, and diviners,
And the prophets throughout all time in
    Babylon, Judah, and Egypt, —
Zoroaster, Maimonides, Enoch, Isaiah,
    Ezekiel, and all.
To the Christ I whispered, too, and 't was
    He alone that repulsed me.
'Tempter, avaunt !' He cried. And so
    He died on the cross.

"Come walk in the garden of know-
    ledge,
In the garden of joy and of knowledge,
    And all that you ask shall be given,
And none of the secrets of life shall
    longer be hidden from you."

Starting up from my sleep with a scream,
    I cry,
What is it ? Where is it ? Speak ! An-
    swer !
And nothing is there but a dream,
    A wild and horrible dream.

She. That is a wild kind of thing, and
is really something like a dream. The
only difficulty is that it is rather too con-
secutive. In our dreams all things seem
to have a natural sequence, though they
are, in fact, utterly dislocated, and so look
to us when we wake.

He. What do you make of madness, —
which seems to be only a dream, or set
of dreams, embodying themselves in the
facts of inner and outer life, from which
the patient cannot free himself, and
awake ?

She. Yes ; and it is difficult to draw
the exact defining line between madness
and sanity. When does the one overstep
the line into the other ? We all of us,
even the sanest, have some hallucina-
tions, called sometimes oddities. We all
of us are insane in our dreams, and make
excursions into the insane and unreal

world of fantasy. A touch of fever, for instance, and the patient goes, as we say, out of his head. But what is his head, and where does he go ? So long as that fever lasts at a certain grade, what he sees, what he does, is to him as real as it is unreal to us. I remember once I had a violent typhoid fever, and for some ten days was quite out of my head. All the real persons around me were phantoms ; all the phantoms of my brain were, on the contrary, real and substantial, — at least to me. There was, for instance, one little dwarf-like figure which constantly attended me, and my mother, who stood at my bedside, was scarcely more than visionary, while this little figure was perfectly distinct and real. One day he perched himself upon my pillow at the right side of my head, and, after leaning over, and looking at me, and grotesquely smiling, he drew out from under his arm a large portfolio, which he spread before me, and slowly turned over its pages as I gazed at them. What that book contained of wonderful and beautiful, ay, and of natural and possible, as well as of strange and indescribable, it is impossible for me to tell. But at every leaf he slowly turned there appeared a new scene; not only the picture of a scene, but a real scene. One I remember in particular was the interior of a vast cathedral, magnificent with columns, and frescoes, and altars, and statues, and thronged by crowds of worshipers, among whom I wandered; and all the while a deep, solemn music was going on, and exquisite voices were sounding in grander strains than ever Handel or Beethoven composed. And this was before I had ever been in a great cathedral. Pictures, too, at that time decorated the bare walls of my chamber, more beautiful in tone and color than ever Leonardo, or Titian, or Raffaelle painted. These were not mere reminiscences or evocations from memory, for I was very young at that time, and had never been in any of the great churches, and cathedrals, and galleries. Afterwards, when years had passed by, what I did see in them seemed to me to recall the visions that in that fever book before me rose so vividly. How will you explain this?

He. Why do you constantly ask me to explain what is entirely inexplicable to me, to you, to everybody ? I, too, have been in the land of fever, and a wonderful region it is, beyond experience, and thronged with the strangest and wildest creations of fancy, — hideous, horrible, fearful, beautiful. Here are some verses that in this connection may interest you. They were addressed to a great traveler, a friend of mine, and in a morbid fit of jealousy at all the wonders he recounted and described, I taunted him thus : —

You have put a girdle round the earth,
　You have traveled far and wide,
From the Orient, where our morning
　　rises,
　To the sunset's western side.
You have trodden the wastes of the African desert,
　And basked in the Tropic's spice,
And climbed the peaks of the Himalayas,
　And been locked in the Arctic's ice.
And I, a short week on my sick couch
　　lying,
　Have journeyed farther still,

To a region wild, and weird, and won-
   drous,
   Where phantoms wander at will.
It was but a moment's sudden parting ;
   Fate opened the door to me,
And this world vanished, and I was car-
   ried
   To regions of mystery ;

Out of the real world about me
   Into a world of dream,
Into the strange world of delirium,
   Where horrors and splendors teem ;
Where Afrites, and Ginns, and Spirits
      wander,
   And wishes and hopes have wings,
And dizzy imagination riots
   And plays with the shapes of things ;

A wonderful world, — ah ! far more
      wondrous
   Than any that here we see,
Where the brain works out wild,
      strange creations
   And creatures of fantasy ;
Where everything shifts, and moves, and
      changes,
   Respondent to thought and whim ;

Where the body is left behind, and the
    spirit
Whirls through a realm of dream;

A realm that lies on the verge of mad-
    ness,
Where the mind no helm obeys,
But helpless, beyond the reach of reason,
    Is swept through delirium's maze ;
Where all that is glorious and ideal,
    And all that is fearful and wild,
Throng gathering round us, to jeer,
    shriek, jabber,
    Or whisper in voices mild.

Abysms of horror there gape before us,
    Impossible monsters arise,
And forms angelic, and struggling crea-
    tures
With glaring and spectral eyes.
Oh, you who for years and years have
    journeyed
    To the ends of this fair earth, say,
Have you seen this world that I traveled
    over
    While here on my bed I lay ?

She. Well ! had he ?

He. No, he had not; and I towered over him exultant, and waved my sword for victory, and, I am sorry to say, stopped him short in one of his best stories. Whether it was founded on fact or not is a question. Travelers' stories are notorious. A man that cannot shoot a pea-gun at a fly at home does such terrible ravages among tigers and elephants in the east, and south, and the wilds of Africa. "There I was, all alone, and five hundred tigers came down upon me, roaring for food. Fortunately, I had with me my patent five-barreled, self-loading and priming gun. You should see that gun, my boy! I believe there is not such another in the world. As this wild band of tigers rushed at me, I stood firm as a rock, and took deliberate aim at the foremost group, and in less than a moment one hundred of them groveled on the sand in their death struggles," *et cetera, et cetera, et cetera.* There is no computing how many lions and tigers one tremendous traveler will dispose of in a minute; nor how many thousand dancing-girls, with cymbals and tambourines, waving their twinkling arms covered with

bracelets, — creatures beautiful as Houris,
— will suddenly appear, when, idly repos-
ing in his Oriental tent in the deserts of
Weiss-nicht-wo, he claps his hands lazily;
nor how many sherbets he can drink ;
nor how many camelopards he can ride.

She. And was your friend one of those
long-tailed Bashaws ?

He. No ; he was not. He was as brave,
good, modest fellow as ever trod on
earth. All that stuff I have been talking is mere rodomontade and nonsense.
There was no exaggeration about him,
and no pretense. He was an English
officer, who spent several years in India,
whose word was as good as an oath, —
better, too, than most oaths. He told
me he made the acquaintance there of a
young fellow, — he did not tell me his
name ; in fact, he thought he went under
a name that was not his own. Something
had happened to him ; my friend never
knew what, but he always suspected that
he had had an unfortunate love affair. At
least, he gathered it was so from words
that the young fellow occasionally let fall.
He never said anything about his family.
In fact, who he was and where he came

from was enveloped in a haze that my
friend never penetrated. One night he
was summoned by an orderly (I think
that's what he called the man) to the
young man's tent, and he found him
alone and dying. Of course my friend
at once said he must call the surgeon or
physician. But the young man absolutely
refused to allow him to do this, saying
that nothing could be done for him, and
he wished nothing to be done for him,
and only prayed him to stay with him
and listen to him. And what he said I
have put into verse, as well as I could.
It was this : —

Bend down your head to me,
My voice is almost gone.
Say ! are we quite alone ?
Yes ? Quite ? Prop up my pillow, —
    wipe my brow !
Ah ! I am easier now.
Thanks ; I am dying, as you see, —
Dying afar from all whom once I knew
And once I loved — save you.

No ! no ! 't is useless — all you say, dear
    friend.
This is, thank God, the end.

They are all happy there,
Who, in their hearts, could really care
 Whether I live or die.
Years have gone by
Since they have seen me — thought of
 me, perhaps ;
And after this long lapse,
Even if perchance they still
May think at times, Is he now well — or
 ill ?
'T is but a passing thought that flies
Like to a bird that flits across the skies,
And vanishes, and leaves no trace be-
 hind ;
'T is but a rustle of the wandering wind
That shakes the leaves a moment, and
 then dies.

Let no one of them know
That I am dead. 'T is better so !
Far better. If they ask about me, say
You met me here, and I was on my way
To a long journey ; that I could not
 write ;
That it was late at night,
And before morning I was forced to go ;
 It will be surely so.
Give them my love and greetings ; say,
 as well,

That whether, where I go, the means
    there be
To send them news of me
    I cannot tell.

The country is so far and strange, I fear
There are no means to send to them from
    there
Tidings of where I am; and tell them,
    too,
I'm ill at writing, even at the best,
And if they hear not from me, they must
    rest
Secure, at least, that I am well to do, —
    Pray God that this be true!

Thus much to all my real friends; for
    why
Obscure their happiness, or make them
    sigh,
Who hold me still dear in their memory,
    If any such there be?
Let them go on and think of me as one
Who still is wandering far away, alone,
But who, some day, again may come
    Back to his friends and home.

But to one only tell the truth, for she
Has been the cause of all the misery

That now for dreary years has haunted
    me.
There is my real name — there in that
    book ;
And there is hers as well, beneath it —
    look !
And there's her face, so cruel, cold, and
    fair.
If you should chance to meet her, say
    to her
You saw me die, death-stricken by the
    dart
That she thrust cruelly into my heart,
Whose poisonous barbs have ever rankled
    there,
And driven me from the world in my
    despair,
And cursed my life ; that I have sought
    for Death —
Wooed him in battle, in the cannon's
    breath,
By sea, by land — ay, wooed him like a
    bride,
And Death, like her, has always turned
    aside,
And laughed at me, as she did ; but at
    last
He comes to free me from the torturing
    past.

I would forgive her if I could.   I pray
I may forgive her ere I pass away.

Tell her all this.   Oh, do not fear !
She will receive it calmly, with a smile
Cold as a gleam upon an iceberg, while
You faltering utter it.   But make her
       swear,
Ere these last words of mine to her you
       bear,
To keep the secret hidden in her breast.
Be sure it never will disturb her rest,
'T is but another scalp for her to wear,
Another bird, another butterfly,
That for her pleasure writhing had to
       die,
That she might grace with it her lus-
       trous hair.

No, my dear friend, I am not cruel.   No,
Far from it !   Do you think that she will
       grieve
One moment, have one pang, one tear
       will shed ?
Never !   You 'll see.   She will receive
With joy the happy news that I am dead,
And dance the next dance with a lighter
       tread, —

If anything upon her heart could weigh,
Perhaps the thought of me,
Living, might trouble her.   Perhaps, I
　　say,
I know not, — and if so it be,
My death, the assurance I have passed
　　away
Beyond all reach, all possibility
Of speech or of return, might lift from
　　her
The faintest breath of trouble, that might
　　stir,
Perchance — who knows ? — some sleep-
　　ing memory
Far down within the heart, — if heart
　　there be
In that cold nature — cruel, cold, and
　　hard,
That all my life so fatally hath
　　marred, —
And from the dead past set her wholly
　　free.

She. That is a sad enough story.   Did
he ever deliver that message ?   And how
did she really take it, if he did ?   Did he
ever tell you what her name was ?   Did
you ever see her ?   What was her name ?

He. Ah, *that* I promised not to tell, and a promise is a promise, and particularly a promise to a dying man, you know.

She. But you did n't make any such promise ; at least, you did not say so.

He. No, I did not say so ; I only told you what he said, not what she said.

She. I don't believe one word of the story from beginning to end. You invented it all to account for your poem.

He. I am sorry you have so little trust in me. And why, may I ask, don't you believe it to be founded on fact ?

She. Because, in the first place, you never can trust to what poets say, as a general rule ; and in the next place, because I don't believe any man ever died of love, except, of course, in poems and romances. It takes a good deal to kill a man. I dare say your poor fellow, if he ever existed, may have been disappointed in his love affair — if he ever had one — and did not like being thrown over, and went about mooning and moaning a little while ; but as for dying of love, no ! Sir Poet, no man ever did. I dare say he wore his collar down, and sulked, and posed for a time, and read Byron's poems and all that, and wandered out into the woods alone, and made bad verses, and sighed, and drank too much wine, but there it ended.

He. This is painful for a poet to hear, — very painful. It saps one's trust in humanity.

She. No ; but you know that you did really delude me at first about your young man, you told his story so seriously. However, we have had enough of him, and now you must read me something more lively, more sentimental, to take the taste out of my mouth, as it were.

He. One moment ; I found in my friend's pocketbook a few verses, which, I suppose, were addressed to that young woman, and I must read them to you. Really, you know, they were rather like her.

She. Like what you fancied she was, you mean.

He. No ; like her, as I knew her.

She. Well, let me hear them.

He.

You spoil my life, you break my heart ;
    but then,
What matters that to you ?

You 've done the same to twenty other
    men,
It is not even new !

To you 't is only what is new that moves
    A moment's interest ;
All that is old — old joys, old pains, old
    loves —
Are birds of last year's nest.

So, with a heartless smile you turn away
    From my impassioned words,
And 't is as if a hand should strive to
    play
A harp that has no chords.

She. I 've no doubt he bored her to
death with his impassioned words.

He. No ; I knew her well. She was a
born flirt.

She. You knew her ? You just said
these lines you found in your imaginary
friend's portfolio. Do be careful.

He. I mean, of course, that he found
these verses, not I, in his friend's portfolio.

She. And how did you come to know
her, pray ?

He. Oh, I won't be examined and cate-
chised. Are you jealous of her ?

She. Yes, I am. I am nothing, if not
frank.

He. But you know a hundred such
women, without particularizing one.

She. No ; only men know such women.
But read me something pleasanter, —
about some nice person.

He. Wait a moment. I want to read
you first a little poem about one of these
women, as you call them, no better in
heart, or feeling, or even morals, than
they should be. They are verses from
the book of a young man whom one of
them had bound and carried at her char-
iot wheels for years ; who had become at
last thoroughly disgusted with her, and
yet who was still her slave, and wanted
strength of will to break away, so fet-
tered was he by old habits and old promises from which he was utterly unable to
free himself.

She. A nice young man, truly.

He. Ah, the difficulty was that he was
not nice, in the real sense of the word, —
which we have now lost ; and more, he
was utterly weak of purpose, and, though

he knew the way, he could not take it.
But you will see, perhaps, what he was
in these verses : —

She has ruined my life, — that is all,
   And almost I hate her, but still
The old spell remains to enthrall
   My spirit and weaken my will.
The grace and the charm of the past
   Have vanished, — that lured me like
      fate, —
But a net o'er my life she has cast
   That is woven of love and of hate.

The old habit, alas ! is a chain
   Whose links I can never undo,
And to break them I struggle in vain, —
   I am weak, all so weak, through and
      through.
I would leave her, and flee, if I could, —
   Life and duty call on me to go,
But I cannot ; I know that I should,
   But I cannot ; I 'm chained to her so.

Ah, well !   'T is my fate, I suppose,
   And 't is useless to strive and rebel,
Though this life now, that once was all
      rose,
   And half heaven, is simply half hell.

Oh ! a curse on the day we first met,
  Though our love was like heaven at
    first,
And its sweetness I cannot forget
  Even now, though my life it has
    cursed.

I 'm a coward; I dare not to say
  Farewell ! Here 's the end ! Let us
    part !
She would storm at me, weep, rave, and
    pray,
  And cry I was breaking her heart.
O God, how the glory and grace,
  How the joy and the fragrance have
    gone !
All the light gone that once lit that face,
  Blown out as a candle is blown.

Nothing left but the smoke and the
    smell
  Of the wick, while in darkness I
    grope
Some outlet to find from this well
  Where I see not one gleam of a hope.
Though myself I revile, and revile·
  Her also, and cry like a fool,
Making bold resolutions the while,
  And striving my weakness to rule.

Well, well ! there 's one outlet alway,
  One remedy — death — if no more.
Here it is. Courage ! What will she say
  When she finds me stretched dead on
    the floor ?
'T is a coward's resource, well I know,
  But I 'm weary, so weary of life,
And perhaps it is best I should go,
  And end all its struggles and strife.

But I dare not. I know if I stay
  These chains I shall nevermore break.
Life 's a torture, but death — ah ! that
    way
  Is too fearful — too fearful to take.
And what would she care if I did ?
  Would she weep or lament ? Would
    she shed
One tear on my cold coffin lid ?
  Would she feel one regret for the
    dead ?

Perhaps ; but what matters it all
  If she does or does not ? Some re-
    morse
She may feel, and perhaps may recall
  The old days as she stands by my
    corse.

But I shall not hear her, thank God ;
  I, at least, shall be free and at rest.
And she 'll find, when I 'm under the
    sod,
  Some new bauble to hang on her
    breast.

She. Well, a poorer kind of weak creature than that I never knew. He could not even make up his own mind what to do, and he did n't know even what he wanted.

He. I don't recommend him to you as so noble and high-minded a being as the rest of us are. But you see that is the wretched condition to which some of your sex reduce some of ours ; for, unwillingly, I am forced to admit that there are some of our sex who are weak and poor things, and some of yours who do not come entirely up to the grand and pure ideals of life that we sometimes form of them.

She. But, after all, these despairing and blighted beings of whom you have given me specimens are only rare exceptions in life, if they ever exist. Now, please let me hear something of a more genial turn of thought and feeling. I don't at all believe in these misanthropes of yours. But whether they exist or not, I should like to leave them for a pleasanter company. Have n't you a poem of a kindlier character to read me ?

He. Yes ; I confess that I agree with you. We have had enough, and more than enough, of these fellows, and to shift the scene, let me read you some lines that Charley wrote to Annie on his return from the Indies. He was a young fellow full of life and hope when he went away. But when he returned, after many years' absence, he had grown to be an old fellow, with white beard and hair, and pleasant ways, and a large fortune. His cares and struggles were over, and he had come home to the old places and the old friends to pass the remainder of his life. One of his first visits was to Annie, with whom he had flirted in his youth, and of whom he had preserved in his heart, like rose-leaves in a book, many a half-tender memory. And this is what he said to her at their first meeting after his return : —

Since last we met how many a long, long
  year
 Hath flown away, with ne'er returning
  flight !
And now your face brings back those days
  so dear,
 That glow in memory with unfading
  light.
We both are changed ! Still, on your
  face I see
 The same sweet smile; the same sweet
  tones I hear ;
The same sweet ways that so enchanted me
 When we were young and glad, without
  a fear.

Ah, me ! you say. Changed, changed,
  indeed, old friend !
 Nothing is now as once it used to be.
No ! Time to you hath had the power to
  lend
 An added grace to that of memory ;
A grace that only time and age can bring,
 A twilight grace that noon nor morning
  knows, —
A tenderer charm, that comes when even-
  ing's wing
 Its softening veil across all nature
  throws.

With laughter once we greeted every
    day,
    And now we greet it with a silent
        sigh !
Yes, we were once more glad and freely
    gay,
    But were we happier in those days
        gone by ?
Through memory's mists — half real and
    half dream —
    Seem they not sweeter than in fact they
        were ?
As the steep cliffs of distant mountains
    seem,
    Their rude facts veiled in mysteries of
        air.

Our hopes are fewer, but are calmer
    far ;
    We ask for less, and we have gained
        content.
No wild desires our peaceful visions
    mar ;
    Life is a simpler plain, of less extent ;
We know at last that youth's wild dreams
    were vain,
    And o'er life's lesser round we peace-
    ful go,

Taking what comes, and not with eager
    strain
  Striving for what life cannot give be-
    low.

What though your hair is white, — I like
    it so ;
  Softer it seems — more delicate — and
    rhymes
More truly to the tender soul I know
  Than those dark curls you wore in
    olden times.
Nay ! do not smile and shake your head,
    my friend,
  'T is really so, — I simply speak the
    truth.
Too old for flattery ? Ah, but I pre-
    tend
  Old age can be even lovelier than
    youth.

You are bound up with all those olden
    days,
  Their joys and pains, their sorrows,
    cares, and dreams ;
And o'er your head an aureole softly
    plays,
  Lit by the light of far memorial gleams.

We have grown old together ; we can
    hear
From far-off time the bells of memory
    ring —
Some sadly faint, some joyous, loud, and
    clear —
That of the past in sweet accordance
    sing.

She. I must confess these reminiscences make me sad. Pray read me something of a different character at once.

He. Well, then, absolutely to change the whole course of thought, I will read you what I call my battle hymn.

She. That will be a change, for there was little that was stirring in the characters you have just drawn, — was there ?

He. Now you will expect trumpets and drums, I suppose, and triumph and shouts and roar of cannon.

She. Of course I shall, as you call it a battle piece.

He. And perhaps you will be disappointed. However, such as it is, here it is : —

BATTLE HYMN.

Grant us, O God, to crush our enemies
That serried round us in battalions rise
    On every side ;
That we may trample them beneath our
    feet
Despite their strength and pride.
Grant us the victory, — victory is sweet,
    Sweet at whatever cost.
Though we be wounded, stricken even to
    death,
Still we will praise Thee with our dying
    breath ;
So that the cause we fight for is not
    lost.

    Anything give us but defeat,
    Anything urge us to but base retreat.
We seek not ease or peace or truce with
    these,
      Our mortal enemies,
But only triumph, — victory at the last,
When the dread conflict shall be past.
Oh, in this battle be our great ally ;
Command us, and we will not fear to
    die.

And where and who are these
Against whose hosts Thy mighty aid we
　　ask ;
Who are our bitter enemies,
Whom to subdue is man's severest task ?
　Behold they all around us stand,
　Within, without, on every hand,
Marshaled by one great leader, — Thy
　fierce foe,
Who fain the hosts of heaven would over-
　　throw,
　　And all the angelic band.

Self-love his armies are, and low desires,
And evil thoughts lit by unholy fires ;
Greed, envy, passions violent and strong;
Revenge, wild impulses to wrong,
Hatred, and cruelty, and sullen will
That longs to wound, — even though it
　　dare not kill ;
Mean jealousy that all but self derides,
And pallid cowardice that skulks and
　　hides,
　　And heeds not duty's call ;
Black falsehood tempting with insidious
　　wiles,
And masked hypocrisy that ever smiles
　Falsely on one and all.

This is the mighty band
That leaguered round us stand,
Against whose fierce attacks and am-
bushed snares
We call upon Thee with our earnest
prayers
To lend Thy helping hand.

Nor these alone. Against the siren
power
Of sweet, seductive passions make us
strong ;
For as we toil with weary oar
The sea of life along,
They ever sing from off a dreamy shore
Their sweet, alluring song.
Come ! come ! they cry to us, and toil no
more.
Here are sweet winds, and happy bowers
of rest ;
Here is dear leisure for the heart op-
prest,
And flower-enameled meadows, all in
bloom,
That fill the ambient air with faint per-
fume.
Give o'er, give o'er
This endless strife of ever laboring life,

And dwell in peace with us, — oh, this is
    best.
Here love lies sleeping ; here are bliss-
    ful dreams,
Lulled by the lapse of ever murmuring
    streams.
    No strife, no toil is here to spoil
The languid luxury of peace and love
In the green earth below, or the blue
    heavens above.

Oh, bind us to the mast, and seal our
    ears,
    For sweet, too sweet, are these alluring
        strains.
    Let Duty's trumpet sound, for in our
        veins
The blood flows stagnant, courage ebbs
    away
While thus we listen.   We are filled with
    fears,
And ah ! we fain would stay.

But we for other lands beyond are
    bound ;
    Here we must not delay.
    The battle must be fought, and not a
        day

Must here be lost. So let the trumpet
    sound,
That all these siren voices may be
    drowned ;
    Let us away.
Courage, no shrinking, each to do his
    part ;
Steady, and forward with an earnest
    heart,
And victory, O God, to ours, we pray !

She. Well, I confess this is not what I
expected from a battle hymn.

He. But is it not one ? What battles
are severer than those which we have
with the enemy within ?

She. I admit the battle is stern, the
victory difficult and doubtful.

He. I have got somewhere here, if
I remember rightly, not a battle hymn,
but a battle speech, which, if you are
disappointed in this, may interest you.
It is a little speech by Captain X. on
board the Victory, let us call her, before
the battle with the Spanish Armada.

She. Oh, yes ; let me hear that.

He. It is on rather different lines
from the other, but you know it is, —

as far as I can remember it — what he really said ; and, by the way, that reminds me of a curious fact in regard to the famous signal of Nelson, " England expects every man to do his duty," that I believe is little known.

She. But which, I suppose, you have invented.

He. No ; this is a real fact, — it is, indeed.

She. Well, what is it ?

He. Nelson's original order was to signal these words : " *Nelson* expects every man to do his duty ; " but in the hurry and confusion the signal for " Nelson " could not be found, and that for " England " was substituted.

She. No ! is that really a fact ?

He. I was not present, but so it is affirmed by those who were. But to go back to Drake's fleet. This is about what the brave Captain X. said to his crew : —

Ah, there they are at last !
Give a cheer ;
Nail your flag against the mast, —
Nail it firm, and nail it fast ;
Never fear !

We will give them all they want,
  And more, too,
For all their brag and vaunt.
Let no doubts your spirits daunt,
There is no such word as "can't"
For the brave and for the true.
We are here to-day to do, —
Not to talk, but to do !
But that is nothing new
For a brave good English crew
Such as you, boys, — such as you !

We are here to-day to fight
With all our English might
For God and for the right, —
  And we mean to do it, too, —
And for good old England's cause,
   And its liberty and laws, —
Hearts of oak, boys, hearts of oak, boys,
   Through and through !

Are there any wish for flight ?
   Let them go !
Now 's the moment ; let them speak !

Ah, I thought so ; none so weak
 As would wish from odds to fly
 When we see our enemy.
It is so, boys, is it not ? It is so.

Ay, that 's the cheer I like.
We are ready now to strike,
   Not our flag, though, — not our flag ;
      ah, no ! no !
But to strike with hands and heart,
And to play our English part,
And to teach these Spanish Dons,
By the talking of our guns,
   A lesson that as yet they do not know.

But be steady, heart and brain !
   Fire low, and sweep their decks
With a storm of iron rain ;
Keep cool, — no hurry, — if again
They wish to see old Spain,
   We will send them back to see it —
      from their wrecks !

Ah, my gallant Spanish ones,
   Who have come with brag and boast,
   With your galleons, and your host,
   To threaten England's coast,
Our answer shall be only with our guns.
We will teach you in the end
   That we are not wholly daft,
   And to all your priestly craft
The hearts of English faith will not bend.
   Come what will, and come what may

We mean to have our say,
And to cry it out from shore unto shore,
  Not with voices sweet and low,
But with cannon voice and roar,
And a message from old England as
      they go.
No more bragging. England wants
No idle taunts and vaunts,
But deeds to answer to her call.
  Every tale our cannons tell
  Will be heard in England well,
And echo back from every cliff and wall.

Now, one more cheer, and then
To your work, my boys, like men,
Like true-hearted English men ;
And let each man fight like ten
To conquer if we can — or to fall !
  The time for talk is past,
  And if this hour be your last,
Do your duty, boys, and God be with us
      all.

She. Yes ; that is honest and English,
but it does not sound exactly like you,
does it ?

He. No ; perhaps it is not in my usual
vein. But all men are really fighters at

heart.   I mean, all who are good for anything.   When the fight in us is wanting,
we might as well give it up.

She. But we women are not fighters,
you know.

He. Oh, are n't you ?   I think your sex
stand to their guns as stoutly as ours, and
more obstinately, perhaps.   We fight
when the blood is up, and you stand
steadfastly to your purpose, and will not
yield when the blood is not up.

She. We are obstinate, you mean.
Thank you.

He. Perhaps, a little.   You don't like
to give in, do you?   You like to have
your own way.

She. I don't give in on this point.   Of
course we like to have our way ; who
does n't ?   But you men don't understand
the wear and tear that we women have in
the worries and demands of household
life.   You have fixed and determined
daily duties to which you are bound, and
which are clear before you.   We have all
sorts of little petty inconsecutive irrita-
tions of the household to worry us, and
there is never an end of them.

He. I pity you.   They would kill me,

I confess. But you bear them with equanimity, and are infinitely clever in your disposal of them, and I have only admiration to give you. But now, to change, as we say in the law, the venue, let me read you a poem which I find lying in my portfolio by the side of the other.

She. What is it ? I hope it is not one of those sad ones.

He. No, not very. It is a poem that I am going to write about you after some years have gone by. I shall, of course, a little exaggerate some facts, but that does not matter. I take it that no poet is to be bound down to exact accuracy, but only to what might have been, or what would have been so delightful if it really had been, whether true in fact or not. Is the free spirit of a poet to be bound down to facts ? I mean in after years to read it to your daughter or grand-daughter, and declare it to be a fact, and then she will open her great blue eyes and smile upon me, just as her mother or grandmother did. Or perhaps she will cruelly say, just as her aforesaid mother or grandmother would, " I don't believe one word of it."

She. Well ; let me hear what you will have the audacity to say.

He. I shall premise it by saying, " You know, my dear " (I shall be very affectionate), — "you know, my dear, your mother (or grandmother) was one of the most beautiful and charming of women, and here in this very place " (for it will be here that we shall meet) "she used on summer mornings to sit and smile upon me with that delightful smile, and to jeer at me and what I read to her ; and I, my dear, used to be very foolish then, whatever I may now be, and young, too."

She. You certainly can be foolish enough ; there is no doubt about that. But I don't know whether I do not like your folly quite as well as your wisdom.

He. Wisdom is known of its children, you know.

She. And folly of its father, I suppose. But let us have the poem.

He.

Amid the glad green leaves of spring
  The nightingales are singing,
Their throbbing notes of happy love
  On the fresh morning flinging ;

And, sitting in the garden here,
  Alone, half broken-hearted,
I dream of thee, and only thee,
  And the dear days departed.

When life was young, and love was ours,
  And nought we cared to borrow
Of sad regrets from yesterday,
  Or longings for to-morrow,
We sat beneath these budding trees,
  By nightingales so haunted,
And the whole world love's perfect spell
  Transfigured and enchanted.

Your head you leaned upon my breast
  In gentle self-surrender,
Both hearts were throbbing with one
    pulse
Of passion sweet and tender.
No need was there of words, for words
  Were all too cold and chilling
The perfect bliss of love to tell,
  The inner life of feeling.

Long years have passed — so long, so
    sad —
  Of changeful human weather,
And here alone again I sit

Where once we sat together.
The young fresh hope, the daring joy,
  The infinite love and yearning,
Ah, they are gone ! forever gone !
  To know no more returning.

Yet still the air, the sky, the earth,
  Are haunted by a feeling,
And silent memories, faint as ghosts,
  Through all the air are stealing.
You are not here, — yet all the place
  Remembers your dear presence,
And through the air a whisper runs
  Of tender reminiscence.

The nightingale the self-same song
  That then he sang is singing ;
The same faint odors pierce my sense,
  The past before me bringing ;
A distant dream comes over me
  That sets my pulses leaping,
And you once more beside me here
  The tryst of love are keeping.

I dream you back to life again,
  But ah, 't is only seeming !
And all the while, with weeping eyes,
  I know I am but dreaming.

The voice, the touch, the smile, the hand,
  Are gone that used to meet me.
I turn, — but to embrace the air, —
  You are not there to greet me.

She. That is very sad, but charming
and touching, — at least to me. What
the world would say I cannot tell, and I
do not care. Let the world go. But are
you not a little ashamed of pretending
that such a poem could possibly be addressed to me ?

He. It might have been. The "might
have beens" are so much more delightful than the realities of life.

She. And so much more painful and
horrible as well. For everything might
have been so much worse, as well as so
much better, than it was.

He. In medio tutissimus ibis.

She. What does that mean ?

He. A friend of mine once translated
it thus : " The ibis is safest among the
Medes." But he was not what you would
call an accomplished Latin scholar, and I
believe it has been interpreted differently
by other and more accomplished scholars,
to mean that the middle way is the

safest ; the mean between too much and too little.

She. It may be the safest, but it certainly is not the happiest. Such a saying is half-brother to " Enough is as good as a feast," which it never is ; a contemptible kind of a proverb. It is a sort of a " while on the one hand, yet on the other hand, nevertheless," or " there is much to be said on both sides," kind of shilly-shally saying. Some cold, horrid, calculating, commonplace creature invented them all. You remember Coleridge's lines ? —

" The certainty that struck Hope dead
  Hath left Contentment in its stead,
   And that is next to best," —

not certainly best, but next to best.

He. Do you think everybody should have an opinion about things in general or things in particular ? A good deal of what I hear in life amounts to about this : —

— What is your opinion, dear ?
— I don't know ; what is yours ?

— I don't know ; what is the general opinion ?

— I don't know ; but I suppose it is what everybody says.

— And nobody thinks ?

— Or perhaps what some one says, and everybody repeats.

— Without thinking ?

— Of course.

She. I am afraid there is some truth in that. It is astonishing in life how a hint, a word, an accidental statement, or a willful misstatement, or a mere guess, or question, or playful allusion, uttered by one person in spite or jest, will grow and grow until it pervades society and becomes a fact believed in by all. Out of one little seed a gigantic upas-tree will expand until it covers and poisons the world.

He. And so in history, — how many facts universally accredited will not bear examination ; but, after all, what difference does it make ? What is the use of bothering one's head about it ? And this, by the way, reminds me of an incident that occurred to a friend of mine, in every way a remarkable as well as a charming and beautiful person, of high education and noble manners. She had a son who, from capriciousness and obstinacy, and the Lord knows for what other reasons (we will not go into them here), chose to marry a handsome but utterly illiterate Italian peasant. After the deed was done the mother had to submit, as all mothers must to the willful whims of their children, and to make the best of it. Shocked at the entire ignorance, even of the history of her own country, her daughter-in-law showed, one day she gave her a brief account — very brief, naturally — of the lives and history of some of the ancient emperors of Rome. The daughter-in-law, after listening for a while, and gaping at intervals, finally said, as a comment on their lives : " Erano cattive genti ! " (They were wicked people !) "Si, cara mia, cattivissime " (Yes, my dear, very wicked), was the mother's answer. " E dove sono adesso ? " (And where are they now ?) asked the daughter. " Dove sono ? Ma son morte secoli fa " (Where are they now ? Why, they have been dead for centuries), said the surprised mother. " Allora," said her daughter, " se erano cattive genti, e se sono tutte morte, non ne pensiamo più " (Then, if they were all bad, and are all dead, don't let us think of them any longer).

She. What a capital way of treating history ! If they were bad and are dead, don't let us think of them any longer. One cannot deny that it is an original view, at least. She must have been a clever girl. Ha, ha ! if they are dead, don't let us think of them any more. Don't let us trouble our heads about them. They can do us no evil, and can do us no good. That exactly accords with what you said a minute ago. What difference does it make whether certain accredited facts in history are well founded or not ?

He. I won't argue with you, for I shall get the worst of it, I know. There is, in fact, very little use in arguing with anybody. After the argument is over, in which both parties ordinarily lose their tempers, the only result is generally that each is more firmly planted in his own view. So don't let us argue. I will agree to anything you say.

She. Well, then, read me another poem, and change the subject.

He. So be it. I have just read you one recalling a morning with you. You profess not to remember *that*, but you certainly will remember that night scene.

She. What night scene ?

He. This is what I said to you ; or no ! it is what you said to me one moonlight evening. Was it in July ? Yes, I think so.

Ah, what a glorious night !
   Here let us linger, love !
The moon with its tender light
   Brims all the heavens above ;
Faintly the dim stars gleam,
   How far in their fathomless deeps ;
And the earth below, in its moonlight
     dream,
   Tranced into silence, sleeps.

Silence is better than words ;
   All we can say is vain ;
For a spirit's touch sweeps over life's
     chords,
   And wakes them to longing and pain.
There 's the sense of an infinite thrill,

Of a whisper that passes by,
Of a haunting mystery, strange and still,
We can only express by a sigh.

Something too much to bear
Is this terrible secret of night.
Lost in the darkness, ne'er
Can thought in its utmost flight
Reach to the end of things.
Onward, onward it goes,
Till weary at last, and with broken wings,
It sinks to the earth's repose.

Our life is a secret, dear,
And a secret 't will ever be.
Who of us mortals here
Can fathom its mystery ?
Love comes — as comes the breeze —
As it will, without our art,
And its blossom wooes from the trees,
And its smile from the human heart.

She. Perhaps I 'll admit that I wrote
that, if you 'll give it to me, and you
won't tell.

He. I shall be only too proud and happy
to give it to you, and I promise you I
won't tell.

She. Why is it that your poems are all so sad ? You are not what I should call a melancholy Jaques in real life. Very much the contrary ; but all that you write has a deep touch of sadness.

He. I do not know. I suppose that far down in the unfathomed silences of all our natures, unless they are simply thoughtless and superficial, there is a prevailing tone of seriousness and sadness. The stream of life only sparkles and bubbles on its surface. The deeps are still, and there the unknown dwells.

She. Yes, I suppose you are right. Even the happiest memories have a touch of sadness, for they are only memories, and not realities, and yet it is a part of my religion that we ought to be happy, and to enjoy the perpetual gifts that God and nature are so generously offering us, instead of repining and longing for what we have not.

He. It is only the follies of human beings that provoke our laughter. Nature never laughs even in her brightest days. At the best, she only smiles, but her smile is a smile of peace. She has violent storms of passion, and deep glooms

of mystery, and darkness, and unfathom-
able silences of feeling ; but she never
laughs out ; at least, so it seems to me.
She is never carelessly gay.   There is
always a feeling of sentiment even in her
happiest moods.

She. But we are always tormenting
ourselves with idle questions, with useless
regrets and longings, instead of enjoying
what God has given.   We are never content with the present.   We yearn for the
impossible, to which we cannot attain,
and the human spirit is never at rest,
whatever we have.   What is distant,
whether in the past or in the future, has
a charm for us which the present never
has.   And yet, what do we own but the
present ?   And ought we not to strive
to enjoy it, and thank God for it ? — at
least, as long as we are oppressed by no
deep sorrows and pains.   I do not believe that God meant us to be wretched
here, and that the only way to heaven is
through self-inflicted sufferings and pen-
ances.   It is hard enough to bear what
we cannot avoid ; but why we should
deny ourselves the delights and enjoy-
ments of life, which are innocent in them-

selves and do no injury to any one, I cannot understand.   On the contrary, I think
the true feeling which should animate
and guide us through life is thankfulness
for what we have.   To say and to believe that all things that delight us and
give us happiness are mere temptations
of the evil spirit is, in my opinion, rank
blasphemy.   I think it is our duty to be
happy and thankful, and to enjoy the
present.

He. Very true.   I agree to all you say,
and somewhere I have a little sermon
upon that text.   Shall I read it to you?

She. Do.

He. Let me see.   Where is it?   I had
it here, I am pretty sure.   Oh! here it
is.

Is it worth while to look upon this world
As mere probation for another state,
Heedless of beauty, scorning all its
   joys, —
Where we are forced to wander and to
   wait ;
Holding its sweetest music but as noise,
And purest pleasures but the devil's bait
To lure us to the loss of all beyond ;

Deeming we do God's service when with
    sad
And downward eyes we go, and solemn
    gait,
Shaking our heads, and crying, "All is
    sad"?

Ah, no! it is all good, and glad, and
    fair.
Let us give thanks to God for sun and
    air,
And spring and summer, and the golden
    chain
Of the recurrent seasons, and sweet flow-
    ers
Painting the meadows, and the singing
    rain,
And all the beauty of this world of ours
That far surpasses all its grief and
    pain!
What if those sorrows and those pains
    there be;
Why dwell alone on them? Look up and
    see
The overplus is beauty, — gladness, —
    love.
Why see in nature nothing but its
    flaws?

The earth is glad below ; the heavens
    above,
When morning opes its gates, or evening
    draws
Its splendid curtains in the west, or
    night
Sows the fair heavens with constellated
    light,
Or the wild winds and tempests, strong
    and free,
Sound the grand organ pipes of har-
    mony,
And bend the forests, and arouse the
    sea,
And shake the world ; or, with a thun-
    der tone,
Drive the black clouds, all seamed with
    lightnings, on,
Lifting at last to show more clear, more
    fair,
The freshened earth, — the invigorated
    air,
In all its cloudless, calm serenity.
Should we prefer one flat monotony
Of ceaseless sunshine to this wondrous
    range
That Nature plays with her perpetual
    change ?

Let us be happy, then, and, grateful, take
What God hath given, — not weep, and
    sadly wail,
But, with a spirit eager and awake,
Seek for the beauty of the world, and
    spread
To every breath of joy the spirit's sail ;
Doing the work that here to us is given
With hearts of gladness, and not holding
    life
As toil alone, and task, and endless strife
Of dull probation for an after heaven.

It is the eye that sees that makes things
    bright
Or dull and dark. The world is what
    we are :
Dark in our darkness, glorious in our
    light.
Love can enchant with beauty infinite
The dullest facts, and sorrow or despair
The sunniest perfectness of Nature
    blight.
Then, since the world our spirit's life
    must wear,
Be it our duty not to mourn and weep,
But evermore a glad, free heart to keep,
Feeling that joy and love are each a
    prayer,

And when the earth looks ugly to our
  eyes,
'T is God, the Maker, that we criticise.

She. Yes, it is, as you say, a little sermon, and might profit some of us, if anybody is ever profited by sermons. You
might take as a text, " Tongues in trees,
books in the running brooks, sermons in
stones, and good in everything."

He. Yes, and thus " translate the stub-
bornness of fortune " —

She. "Into so quiet and so sweet a
style " —

He. No, No! Into so preaching and
so tame a style, I should rather say, and
I am sure my critics would.

She. No matter what your critics would
say. As for me, I agree fully with the
substance of your little sermon, but it is
not always easy to be happy, whatever
our duty is. And we ought, as you say,
to enjoy the present, and not always be
looking back and regretting, or forward
and hoping.

He. But, — there is always a but to
every proposition, — but however we may
pretend to live in the present, in fact we do

not ; we live in what is past and in what
is to come, — or what we think is to
come, — far more than in what we have.
Here are a few insufficient lines on this
subject : —

None are ever content with the present,
   Though the present only we own :
Age is forever looking backward
   To the days and the things that are
      gone,
And youth is forever stretching forward
   To the joys that are coming on.

Yet all that we really have is the present,
   And that flees from us so fast
That, cling to it as we will, we lose it, —
   While we speak, it is lost and past.
For all things are ours but a single mo-
      ment,
   And scarcely that moment last.

Almost we might say that what is van-
      ished
   Alone is ours to keep,
For nothing can change or steal it from
      us
   Till memory falls asleep.

Even fate itself has no power to change
    it,
Or death with its sickle to reap.

She. True, true. The past is ours, ir-
revocably ours ; the present is but a running stream, the future a vague promise.
But whatever is, is, and who knows anything ? But a truce to these sad thoughts.

He. I know but one exception to the
general rule of discontent that is almost
universal, and that is in a little stunted
figure of a woman I see daily as I go
to my work, who reads me ever a silent
lesson by which I hope I profit. Nature and the world have denied her the
gifts we all covet, and yet, apparently,
her heart has taught her to take content-
edly what has been given, small and poor
as it is. The other day I wrote these
lines about her : —

No outward things can happiness bestow,
  'T is born within; we give what we
    receive.
The spirit o'er life's dreariest road can
    throw
  Joy's light, the brightest of that joy
    bereave.

What, hapless maid, did God confer on
    thee
Of what all mortals covet and desire ?
Health — beauty — wealth — the world's
    prosperity ?
    Or even the gifts that humblest lives
    require ?

Nothing ! a dwarfed, diseased, and
    stunted form
    He gave. Pain, poverty, is thine, —
    and want ;
No grace without, and yet, within, a
    warm
    And patient spirit angels seem to
    haunt.

Poor, unrepining, plain, — but rich in
    heart
    To cheer dull Duty's daily common-
    place
And sweet content, Life's hardest, happi-
    est art,
    That even to rudest facts can lend a
    grace.

When o'er thy face thy smile its magic
    throws,

Plain though thy features are in form
and hue,
It is as if an inward morning rose
And o'er stern cliffs its sudden glory
threw.

Others, by fortune blessed with lavish
dower,
Still covet more, and o'er their lot
lament ;
But thou, in gratitude for life's least
flower,
Art happier far and richer, in content.

There, cold or hot, rain, storm, or cloudless skies,
Patient you sit, your petty wares out-
spread
On the stone steps ; and as I pass you
rise
And greet me with a smile, and nod
your head.

That smile is as a rose for me to wear,
Which lends a perfume to the dreari-
est day ;
A silent lesson, that life's worrying care
Rebukes, and bids me for contentment
pray.

She. You must show me this woman.

He. Gladly. When I think how miserable is her lot, and still what a bright and happy face she has despite it all, I feel deeply rebuked for my vain longings and dissatisfaction with what I have. Ah, yes, the lines of Coleridge are true to her, that we were quoting a few minutes ago : —

"The certainty that struck hope dead
  Hath left contentment in its stead."

And perhaps *that* is not only, in her case, next to best, but best.

She. Well, well ! All I have to say is that the world is what we make it. But now let us have something of a lighter, gayer sort, — something with a little less sadness and retrospection, and more go.

He. A gallop, for instance.

She. Oh, yes ! A gallop in the fresh air and the fresh morning. Pray order the horses at once. The very word "gallop" makes my blood tingle and spin to the ends of my fingers. But I know you. You only mean to taunt me. You have no such poem.

He. Oh, but I have, may it please your highness, and the horses are saddled and ready, and gnawing at their bits. One spring, — give me your foot (I do not dare to ask for your hand). There, and now are you ready?

She. Quite, and impatient to be off.

He. And where shall we go ?

She. Anywhere ; you shall lead the way.

He. And you will trust to my guidance ?

She. As long as you behave yourself with sanity.

He. Oh, I cannot promise to be sane, galloping with you at my side. You must take leave of the flat plains of sanity, if you accept me for a guide ; for I shall carry you far beyond them, into the regions of dreams and wild wishes.

She. Well, mount your horse at once and let us be off.

He. All right, gather up your reins, and

Come, let us gallop, gallop along !
  'T is so golden sweet this early May,
The hedges and trees are alive with
    song,

And heaven is thrilled by the lark's
　　far lay.
Our horses are fresh.　How they sniff
　　the air,
　　And spread their nostrils, and snort
　　　and neigh !
Come, love, let us be off and away,
And fling to the foul fiend every care.

Ah, how glorious 't is !　How glad
　　Nature seems to be all at play !
'T would be almost a sin to be dull and
　　sad
　　On a day like this, — such a glorious
　　　day.
Since we cannot fly, let us ride — ride —
　　ride —
　　Whither and where, who cares to say ?
　　Anywhere — everywhere — riding al-
　　　way,
You and I together, side by side.

I don't know why we should ever stop,
　　Why the morning should fade into
　　　evening's gray,
Why life from its grasp youth's flowers
　　should drop,
　　And age on our spirit its cold hand lay.

Time goes ever and ever on,
  Never is weary, knows no stay ;
  And why should not youth be ours al-
    way,
And love, and joy, till our course is run ?

Happiness now is in the air
  And our hearts are young and light
    and gay ;
Let us not darken the morning with care,
  As we gallop along youth's flowery
    way ;
Let us dream it will last forever thus,
  Let us gather our roses while we may,
  And be glad in the present, and silently
    pray
That life may be ever so to us.

Oh, love, what a glory and bloom you
    give
  To the commonest things of every day ;
Now, 't is enough to breathe and live.
  If time and love would together stay,
What could we ask for more sweet and
    fair
  Than thus to go on with youth alway,
  We both together, with love and May,
And the perfume of morning in the air ?

There is only one thought of doubt and
    fear,
That looms from afar, so faint and
    gray, —
Lest we should be parted, and one left
    here,
And the other ruthlessly taken away.
For life is cruel, and fate unkind,
    And what may come to us who can
    say ?
But away with forebodings, for now
    't is May,
And love to such fears must be deaf and
    blind.

She. Yes, that is out of a different
mint ; but, as usual, despite the bright-
ness and spirit, there is that little cloud
on the horizon that one cannot help seeing, — or feeling, at least, if one does not
see, — that faint foreboding, that dark
possibility that will intrude upon our
gladdest hours. Who has ever seen in
life a perfectly clear sky ?

He. Would there be any sentiment in
life without it ? Those little clouds afar
off lend their charm to our being, and
take the tenderest hues of the morning

and of the evening. Life would, perhaps, even at its best, be vapid and mo-
notonous without them. Look at the val-
leys and mountains sleeping below in the
distance, over which soft silence broods.
Is it not the tender haze of blue that
envelops them that lends them their exquisite charm ? Sweep it away entirely,
and what would remain but a cold, hard
reality ?

She. Yes ; Nature in her most poetic
moods always plays in the minor tone.
She never heartily laughs, as you said, and
any laugh, even of gladness, has in itself
something a little jarring in its sound,
from however gay a heart it comes. It
is as closely related to a mere noise as a
smile is to a silent melody. A laugh
simply irritates the nerves ; a smile
touches the feelings.

He. Can anything be less enchanting
than silently to listen to a crowd of gay
people all laughing together, and thinking, or making believe, that they are
happy ? It is all very well when one is
joining in the discordant chorus of spasmodic voices ; but when one stands aloof
from it, and simply listens, what a de-
testable noise it is !

She. So it is ; and it is curious that the animals do not laugh. *That* is the accomplishment of human beings only.

He. I confess that I do not know much about angels, but I do not believe they laugh. At all events, they are never represented as laughing by poets or painters. It is the fiends only that laugh, if we may trust what the poets say.

She. May I look at that manuscript book of yours ?

He. Certainly. There it is.

She. Thanks. Why, here are sketches, as well as poems and notes.

He. Yes, it is an odd collection of all sorts of things. I always carry one of these books in my pocket, so that I may write down anything that occurs to me in my ramblings. You see, here are little sketches of many different things, — landscape, houses, bits of scenery, heads and figures, — as well as scribblings of verses and excerpts from books that I am reading, when the passages particularly strike me. They are mostly very carelessly done, but they serve to recall persons and places, and make for me a little diary of what otherwise would vanish utterly, or at least but dimly remain in my memory. Some of the verses I have read to you, as you will see, are in the portfolio of the book, and I happen to have them with me because I was questioning as to whether it was worth my while to make a little collection of them and publish them, and I took them out here with me the day before yesterday to look them over.

She. Oh, I hope you will decide to publish them.

He. Perhaps I shall ; and then again perhaps I shall not. The pleasure is in the doing. When things are done, — they are done, and dead. I lose my interest in them. It is what I am going to do — or am doing — that interests me, and beckons and allures me on with smiles. What is done only frowns upon me, and sneers at me, and says : "It is not much of a thing, after all, is it ? "

She. That it may seem so to you I quite understand. But the case is different for those who read and hear. If you fail to satisfy yourself, you may give pleasure to others, and I think it is a little selfish in you to keep all these poems to yourself. You ought to publish them.

He. Selfish! Oh, I like that! Selfish, indeed; I should rather say shy or proud, or, still better, modest. You laugh. But really I am modest, and don't like to be slapped in the face, or to expose myself to attack. So long as I don't publish, nobody can attack me. If I once publish, then I am the butt for all the critics. I only wish I could flatter myself with even the suspicion that in withholding these verses from the public I am selfish. My doubt is whether it would think them worth reading at all.

She. You see I do.

He. Ah, but you are a friend, and the public is not a friend; and though the saying is that "you should not look a gift horse in the mouth," the critic, and indeed the world in general, always does look, the moment the horse is given. As for the critics, they always know better than the author what he ought to have done and how he ought to have done it. Their province is to find fault with anything and everything, and show their own superior knowledge and ability. But

somehow or other, when they try it themselves, they don't always show that su-
periority. And besides, though I say it
with fear and trembling, they are not
always so absolutely right as they think
themselves. I won't say anything about
a certain William Shakespeare, or Shak-
spere, or Shaxper, whom the world of
contemporaries patted on the head, ac-
knowledging he was a good fellow, but
shaking their heads sadly and patroniz-
ingly over his works, or accusing him of
" beautifying himself with others' feathers " and " thinking himself the only
shake scene in the country," and wishing
he " had blotted a thousand lines " and
followed their advice. At all events,
some of his great plays, whatever he
thought of them, were never printed or
published by him, but only by others and
long after his death, he being, as you
would say, perhaps, a little too selfish,
or, as I should say, too modest —

She. No ! really !

He. Undoubtedly; and for those that
were printed he seems to have cared very
little. At all events, he allowed them to
be printed in the most careless, imper-

fect, and mutilated form. Such, for instance, was the case with "Hamlet;" and as for "Julius Cæsar," "Cymbeline," "Coriolanus," "Henry VIII.," and "Othello," they were not published until from five to seven years after his death. But, setting aside the "Great Williams," as our French friend called him, look in our own time at the first reception of Wordsworth by the world of critics, and remember the "This will never do" of Gifford on Wordsworth's early volumes. It managed to do, did n't it, after all? And then please to remember what the first judgment of the world was of Keats and Shelley, and compare it with to-day's opinion of their poems. Almost one could say that nothing of really great originality and excellence is ever well received by the world at first. An author has to make his public, and to make it slowly. Not that I would, in the faintest way, presume to imagine that there is anything in common between these poor little things of mine and the works of any really original men such as those I have spoken of. Far from it. The best that can be said of them, even by a

friend, is that they are not so utterly
bad as they might have been ; and *that* is
not any great praise, is it ?   And then,
perhaps, they have a worse fault, — of
being simply commonplace.   And so I
am what you are pleased to call selfish
in keeping them to myself.

She. But is it true, as you say, that
Shelley was not accepted as a poet at
once ?   Wordsworth, I know, was not,
but Shelley, — that is difficult to believe.

He. Well, then, listen to words of his
reviewer in the great "Quarterly Re-
view."   I have them, or some of them,
here somewhere, for I was reading this
criticism the other day, and it amused me
so much that I copied one or two sen-
tences.   Stop a moment, and I will find
them.   Ah, here they are.   The critic in
the "Quarterly" says : "The predom-
inating characteristic of his poetry is its
frequent and total want of meaning ; "
and he describes his "Prometheus" as
"in sober sadness driveling prose run
mad."   But this is nothing compared
with what the critic in the "Literary
Gazette" says of the tragedy of the
"Cenci," which he speaks of as "the

most abominable work of the time;" and he hopes never again to see a book "so stamped with pollution, impiousness, and infamy." As for the "Prometheus," it is, in his opinion, "little else but absolute raving, and, were we not assured to the contrary, we should take it for granted that the author was a lunatic, as his principles are ludicrously wicked, and his poetry a mélange of nonsense, cockneyism, poverty, and pedantry;" and further on he speaks of "the stupid trash of this delirious dreamer," and his "tissue of insufferable buffoonery."

She. I confess I am surprised. I could not have believed this possible. Is this a hoax of yours?

He. No, not at all; it is a plain fact. It is curious to contrast with these expressions the modern estimate of Shelley. William Michael Rossetti, in his memoir of Shelley, says, speaking of the "Prometheus," that in his opinion "there is no poem in English poetry comparable, in the fair sense of that word, to it. The immense scale and boundless scope of the conception, the marble majesty and extramundane passions of the personages, the radiance of ideal and poetic beauty which saturates every phrase of the subject," etc., "form a combination not to be matched elsewhere, and scarcely to encounter competition." "It is the ideal poem of perpetual and triumphant progression." And of the "Cenci" he speaks as "his one unparalleled masterpiece," and as "a splendid performance," which "the soundest and finest minds" are "fully justified in preferring" to the "Prometheus." There is a difference of opinion, is there not? So you see that the first judgment of the world of critics as to poetry does not always coincide with its last.

She. Both, perhaps, are wrong; the one on the side of too little appreciation and the other of too great exaggeration. I don't think I could go so far as Mr. Rossetti in the estimate he places on the "Prometheus" and the "Cenci," glorious as I think some of Shelley's other and smaller poems are. Still, I cannot conceive how anybody could be so blind and self-willed as those old reviewers whose criticisms you have cited. But since you say that nothing very original ever finds at once its public, or is kindly received, it ought to comfort and flatter you if your verses are even rejected at first. You ought to hope that they would not be well received. At all events, I think you should better try it.

He. Well, perhaps I will. Still, you see, provided I keep them in my private portfolio I can indulge myself with all sorts of imaginary ideas about them. While the world outside bustles and cries and fights, I sit in my study and enjoy my seclusion from it all, and am protected from all attacks, so long as I do not expose my life and my verses. But if I go out I must be ready to brave the storm and the gale. Here I sit and enjoy the comforts of privacy, and hold commune with the spirits of the past, or sit over the fire with a friend, and keep my temper, and indulge in all sorts of quiet and peaceful occupations or silent musings. And, apropos, let me recall to you those charming lines you wrote some twenty years or more ago.

She. I must have been very young then to have written any verses, or, at least, any worth reading.

He. Oh, when you wrote these verses you were at least twenty years older than you are now, — or you imagine yourself to be. But you surely remember that you had a cottage by the seaside, and a husband and two children, who were perfect angels, of course; don't you remember?

She. Not exactly ; and, particularly, I don't remember the husband, nor the children, that you say were such angels.

He. Don't remember ! why, you wrote those verses about them, in which you describe an evening in the cottage during a storm, and you know you gave them to me !

She. Well, let me hear them, then. I shall be so glad to make the acquaintance of my husband and children, for I have never seen them, — either of them.

He. Well, this is your poem : —

AT THE FIRESIDE — BY THE SEA-SIDE.

How the wind roars !
How the rain pours,
Pressing with furious gusts the pane,
And lashing against them with streams of
rain
Again, and yet again !

And how black it is outside ! how drear !
    Ah me ! ah me !
I 'm so glad with you to be well housed
    here,
Here, in this peaceful privacy,
So peaceful, so free from fear.

Hark to the tempest, the distant roar
Of the thundering breakers along the
    shore ;
    And think of the sailors out at sea,
Where the wild sea-horses are flinging
    their manes
    To the angry blast, and rearing their
    crest,
    And madly plunging as if possessed
      By the demon of the air,
And sweeping the deck, as their poor ship
    strains
Like a giant, struggling, staggering,
    fighting,
    As the seas against her beat, —
    Almost I can see them there !

Think of them, dear, on this horrible
    night
And here, — so near, — scarcely out of
    sight,

Almost at our very feet,
Hark ! on the cliffs with a wild unrest
How the surf-waves beat and dash their
 breast,
  Storming them fiercely with angry
   sleet, —
Or rushing like charges of cavalry,
And thundering along the beach ! Ah
 me !
For the poor drenched sailors out at sea,
How sad it must be ! How sad it must
 be !
How fearful it all must be !

And for those on shore, crouching down
 to the storm
  That shakes and roars in the groaning
   trees,
'Neath the shelter of hedges, or forcing
 their track
  In the face of the blast, whose wild
   gusts seize
And tear their close-wrapped cloaks
 from their back,
  As stern on their desolate path they
   go, —
Striving and straining, their heads bent
 low,

Longing for home and the fireside
  glow,
And the wife and the children that
  there are at play, —
And the home and the fireside so far
  away !
And the heavens above them so wild and
  black !
While we, well housed and out of the
  storm,
Are sitting together, contented and
  warm ;
With the bright fire glowing, the lamps
  alight,
  And nothing to trouble us two ;
Only in thought going forth to the drear,
Wild tempest outside, with a shudder of
  fear
  And a sympathy, silent, but true,
For all who, unhoused, on this terrible
  night,
For their life, — for their home, — must
  struggle and fight.

Let us be grateful, then, to be here,
Housed and happy, as we are, dear !
Both, both together, beyond the blast,
With nothing to do, and nothing to fear;

To love and be silent, to hope and to
    dream,
Now of the future and now of the past ;
And stretch out our hands to the fire-
    light's gleam ;
I with my knitting, and you with your
    book,
From which you at intervals lift up your
    eyes, —
At times with approval, at times with
    surprise, —
Some passage to read, or to criticise ;
This one to praise, and that to rebuke,
Or say that the world was so far more
    wise
In the good old days ere its ways it for-
    sook ;
Or you go to the window, and, shudder-
    ing, look
Into the darkness that shrouds the skies ;
Or, pacing the carpet, stride to and fro,
Picking its patterns for steps as you go,
Till, tired of pacing our deck, you then
Come back to your chair and your book
    again.

The very tempest that roars outside,
And shakes the shutters with rattle and
    din,

Makes it by contrast more cheerful with-
    in,
As here we sit, so calm and serene,
Whatsoever the outer world may betide ;
Both the children abed and asleep up-
    stairs,
Of the storm's wild fury quite unawares,
And not even disturbed by a dream,
While we, with nought in the world so
    wide
To plague us, are sitting here side by
    side.

But hark ! what was that, — that
    scream ?
Was it theirs — was it theirs ?
Stop ! listen ! ah no ! 't was only the
    wind
Tearing away at the blind.
Thank heaven, it was not their voices.
    No ! no !
But it startled me so ! it startled me so !

She. And those are my verses, you
say. Well, give them to me. If they
were mine, I must have been a delightful, sympathetic old woman, whatever I
am as a young woman.

He. There they are; take them. You
were a charming old woman then, as you
are a charming young woman now.

She. I make you my humblest bow,
or curtsey. But seriously, to return to
what we were saying before. This poem
is all very well as a picture of home comfort, undisturbed by the wild voices of
the outer world. I have nothing to say
against it. Your imagined family — I
mean to say my husband and I — were
undoubtedly right in congratulating ourselves on our comfortable and pleasant
fireside out of the storm. But for any
writer to withhold his works from the
public on such a plea seems to me to
argue cowardice as well as selfishness.

He. As for cowardice, I will not say
that you are not right, or, at least, partially right. The harsh words of the
world affect us deeply, however we admit
their truth and their justice ; ay ! and
more, perhaps, than the kind words of
friends gratify us. So long as we keep
ourselves to ourselves, we are not ex-
posed to this. And, after all, what right
have any of us to expect better treat-
ment than we get, to receive what, I

concede, we desire, — in trembling and doubt perhaps, but still we do desire. Besides, I am not willing to accept the public verdict, or, at least, the first verdict of the world, as to the value of what we do, and that is all I shall ever know. It may be right, or it may be wrong, but it annoys us none the less when it is wrong. As for selfishness, there I make a stand. Even if I am selfish, who is not in this world, and what is not? Our ambition certainly is, and so is our fear, and so is our love. They who are in love think only of themselves.

She. Oh, no! not those who are in love. They look kindly on every person and thing in the world. Love lends a kindly seeing to the eye.

He. Except for those who interfere with their private and personal satisfactions. Lovers all hate the world, and only desire to be alone together. I am afraid I have been talking a little big, and as if I had a certain spite against the world, arising from disappointment or ill-humor, and as not having received my right appreciation from it. But, if so, I have been utterly false to myself. I

have everything, as far as this world
goes, to be grateful for, and nobody thinks
less of his deserts than I do. Bah! but
I will not talk about myself any more.
What I know and think is simply this, —
I have no splendid greenhouses and gorgeous gardens filled with exotics and wonderful flowers. No, no ! —

Mine 's but a kitchen garden
    Of herbs, unpretending and low,
Where marjoram, borage, and basil,
    And sage, and sweet lavender grow.
There is rosemary, too, for remembrance,
    Coriander, mint, dittany, dill ;
And with savory, sorrel, thyme, parsley,
    You your Perdita's basket may fill.

But there is not one stately white lily
    To lend its virginal grace,
Nor a rose, nor a spicy carnation,
    To charm and enchant the whole
        place.
On its wall climbs no delicate jasmine ;
    No sweet honeysuckle is there ;
No ! nor even the tulip, with shaking
        cup,
    Nor camellia, cold and fair.

It is but a humble garden,
  With scarcely a flower to see,
Save some pansies for thought, and some
    violets
  Half hidden, that there may be.
Kind friends may stoop down and gather
    them,
  If there they should chance to stray,
But the world says, They are so com-
    mon, —
  And turns with a sneer away.

No matter! however common
  My little garden of herbs,
It gives me pleasure to plant them and
    till them,
  And no one it harms or disturbs.
They serve, too, life's daily living
  To season, and flavor to lend.
But if they are not to your taste, God
    help us,
  I 've nothing to say, good friend.

There, that 's the way I feel about the
whole matter.

She. Well, I don't find any fault with
it. It is modest, at least, and modesty
is a rare thing to meet with nowadays.

Perhaps you don't quite do yourself justice, but that is better than bragging. "Fire low," you remember, was Cromwell's command to his army. "Trust in God, and fire low." It is good policy, too.

He. Perhaps, though, the world in such cases is very ready to take you at your own estimation. Pretension too often carries the day over real merit and power. It is not always, indeed it is very seldom, that the best and the strongest are set in the highest places.

She. Still, I think everybody finds his true level at last.

He. Do you? Happy and trustful you! I don't agree with you ; at least, I should n't if I dared to disagree.

She. I suppose there is a good deal to be said on both sides, as there always is.

He. It is good policy, you just said, to be modest. I hate the word "policy," and the thing. Honesty may, as it is said, be the best policy, but there is something degrading in being honest for the sake of policy. Let us be brave to say and to be what we really and truly are and think, and not compromise our conscience by lies and pretenses, however politic, for it is a lie to pretend to be what you know you are not. Policy and Expediency, who are twin-brothers, are both of them surreptitious claimants, who are seeking falsely to acquire the rights and property of Honor and Honesty, that do not really belong to them.

She. I fear, if those are your principles of conduct and speech, that you will not get on very far with the world.

He. Perhaps I shall not. I did not say that I should.

She. May I look at that manuscript book of yours again? Are these first drafts of poems, or have you copied them out?

He. Some of them I have taken the trouble to copy out, but for the most part they are just as I wrote them, with all their faults.

She. But in some of them there are scarcely any erasures or corrections.

He. I dare say there is a lot of rubbish.

She. Do you correct and elaborate much?

He. Look for yourself, and you 'll see. Everything depends upon the mood I am in, and whether I am in a free vein. Then things come to me very rapidly; and when this is the case I generally do my best — poor as it is — at first, and I only make what I have done colder by correction. When the mood is gone, the words and thoughts that fit to it go too. One can't, or at least I can not, understand how one can write a poem of " malice prepense," as we say in the law. Thought and feeling should be molten to flow into the mould of a poem, not hammered and filed into shape. I speak for myself only, not for others. I know many poets polish, and change, and elaborate with great fastidiousness. I doubt whether they always, by so doing, better their poems, — if they are real poems. But on this, as well as on all other subjects, there is much to be said on both sides. Mere facility is apt to degenerate into careless and slovenly garrulity, and too much labor and fastidiousness into hardness and coldness. Out of the fullness of the heart the mouth speaketh. The height of the fountain's jet depends on the force and fullness of the upper spring. When the

spirit is alive and earnest it finds its true
expression with ease ; but one cannot
pump up enthusiasm or studiously hunt
out its true and natural language. *That*
comes by instinct, not by study.

She. I should like to see Shakespeare's
manuscript.

He. Should you ? How strange !

She. I mean, to see whether he cor-
rected much.

He. Ben Jonson says he did n't, and
he reproves him for it, and says he would
he had blotted a thousand lines, and that
he went on with too great facility. I
can easily believe Ben blotted a great
many in his own work, but —

She. Oh, no matter about Ben Jonson. Let him go, for the present. Here
is a blank page, — no, not quite blank,
there is a pressed leaf on it, and there is
a name and a date. May I read the
poem there, that seems to refer to it ?
Is it very private ?

He. Read it if you wish. I don't remember anything about it.

She. Oh, poets, poets, what a singular
lot you are ! Well, I shall read your
poem, since you give me leave, and I

shall read it aloud, and you then can tell me what you think of it, if you have really forgotten it.

He. How can I help thinking it the most beautiful of poems if you read it?

She. Don't be foolish. Listen!

A leaf, a name, a date,
   Are all that now remain
Of that glad month, that golden time,
   That ne'er will come again.
Ah, God! how all goes by, —
   Youth, love, joy, — everything
That once gave glory to our life
   In its fresh days of spring.

A faded autumn leaf!
   But at its touch arise
What odors wafted from the past
   Of happy memories.
Thine eyes again I see,
   Thy lips again I press,
Those eyes that looked such love to
     mine,
   Those lips that breathed to bless.

The torrent's murmuring voice
   Goes babbling through the glen;

We lie beside it on the grass,
    Far from the eyes of men.
Our hearts keep fluttering round
    One sweet, delicious theme,
And the happy, childish days go by,
    Like music in a dream.

The blue jay shrills afar,
    And, flashing through the trees,
The oriole, like a gleam of fire,
    Rustles and vanishes.
Across the tender sky
    White cloudlets drift and sail,
And o'er the glowing woods is drawn
    A soft autumnal veil.

Your voice, your tones I hear,
    The very words you said,
And on my breast I feel again
    The weight of your dear head.
Upon the running stream
    That hurries past, we throw
The wild flowers blooming at our feet,
    And idly watch them go.

Nothing comes back again,
    Each moment hurries on,
Gives us a kiss, gives us a stab,
    Greets us, and then is gone.

Nothing is ours to keep,
　　And nothing e'er returns,
Though all the soul, with outstretched
　　　　prayers,
　　Again to grasp it yearns.

Alas ! of all that then
　　Was glad, and pure, as brief,
What now remains ?   This faded flower,
　　This dead autumnal leaf ;
A name, — thy name, — a date, —
　　The date of that dear day, —
And all the rest, like some sweet song,
　　To silence passed away.

Ah, no !   It has not gone,
　　It lives within my heart,
An odor sweet that haunts my thoughts,
　　Preserved by love's fond art.
And oft a touch, a tone,
　　A whisper of the breeze,
A passing scene, brings back again
　　The vanished memories.

Yes, for a moment brings
　　The past, and then again
In the dim vast it vanishes,
　 To leave a thrill of pain.

Fate, with relentless whip,
Lashes the present by,
The future tempts us but to cheat,
The past is one long sigh.

She. There, what do you think of it ?

He. Ah me ! ah me ! ah me !

She. Why, there are tears in your eyes. Forgive me !

He. Oh, I am a fool, I know. But that day was one which I passed with my sister in the woods at B., when we were both young, and both happy, and both trusting. She was half of my life to me. She entered into all my hopes, cheered me in all my ambitions, gave me always the wisest and tenderest sympathy and counsel. She was what only a sister can be, and if there be anything good in me I owe it to her. No one to me can ever fill the gap that she left. But excuse me. I did not mean to talk about myself, and do you know that sometimes you yourself recall the memory of her ? Not that you look like her. No ; but I never wrote anything that I did not read to her, and she thought everything I wrote was remarkable. Dear creature ! She had scarcely the heart to think anything of mine bad, or to depress me by any severe criticism.   And somehow, though you are not in the least like her, and certainly do not exaggerate my merits, the mere fact that I read to you these poor things, and that you are willing to hear them, recalls faintly the old days and the old readings.   I don't think I could quite make up my mind to read these verses to any man.   Men are so cold, and so critical and unsympathetic.   Poetry to them, for the most part, is so outside of their life, so to speak.   As for authors, they are so fixed in their own notions as to what any work should be, that they incline generally rather to criticise than to sympathize, and to think anything could be done better in some other way.   But women always listen with sympathy at least, and are more ready to exaggerate the merits than to weigh the faults and defects of what is read to them.

She. It is, in itself, an implied compliment to any woman when an author, and particularly a poet, reads his poems to her ; let me thank you, as I do most sincerely and heartily, for showing this kindness to me.

He. On the contrary, it is you who have done me the kindness to listen to them so sympathetically. For, you know, it *is* a kindness. An author better understands his own work when he reads it aloud to another. He feels where it comes short, where it fails in conveying the impression he desired. He is able better to criticise it for himself. It assumes a comparatively new form and character to him.

She. I had no idea that I was doing you a favor. I thought it was all the other way.

He. Well, then, we are both contented, are we not?

She. I am, at least; and if you are, you will please prove it by reading another poem. There is one, indicating the different ways in which nature affects different minds, that you promised yesterday to bring and to read to me. Have you brought it?

He. Yes, I have; but now that I look at it, I am afraid it is too long.

She. Well, I will be the judge of that. Come, read it, please.

He. First, let me read you a shorter one, that I see here.

She. Very well, if you like ; but I am not going to let you off from the other, afterwards.

He. This is a little poem to Lesbia.

She. And who is Lesbia ?

He. You will see.

Ah ! lovely Lesbia, through whose eyes
    so blue
  A laughing light looks forth, whose
    pouting lips
Are red as roses moist with morning dew,
  What shall preserve these charms
    from Time's eclipse ?

Must coming years intrench that perfect
    brow
  With cruel lines, these blooming
    cheeks invade,
Where quick the warm blush mounts and
    mantles now,
  And o'er thy glowing beauty cast a
    shade ?

Can nothing save thee from the spoil of
    time ?
  Nothing avert the silent siege of fate ?

Nothing preserve thee in thy perfect
   prime
  As now thou art, and keep and conse-
    crate ?

Nothing but Art — and Art, how vain it is
  For all its vaunt — that can preserve
    alone
Youth's shadowy semblance ere it van-
   ishes
  When youth itself and all its charms
    are flown.

Surer is death ! If in thy beauty rare,
  Thy radiant youth, stern death should
    summon thee,
Thou wouldst remain forever young and
   fair,
  Unharmed by time, embalmed in mem-
    ory.

Ah, then, no change, — no faltering steps
   like ours
  Adown the steeps of life, — Death's
    silent bride
Thou shouldst be crowned with youth's
   perpetual flowers,
  And sorrow from thy pathway step
    aside.

Still, lovely Lesbia, smile, while smile
 you may ;
 Accept life's bounteous gifts while
  youth divine
Scatters its roses on your laughing way,
 And take as tribute one poor poet's
  line.

You 'll read it now with half a smile and
 sneer,
 And lightly laugh, and shake your
  graceful head ;
Well ! — wait ! and read it after many a
 year,
 When you and I are old — or I am
  dead.

Perchance it may recall a distant day,
 A happy hour denied to after years ;
Perchance, — and then, — but wipe them
  quick away
 If in your eyes should brim unbidden
  tears.

What is the use of sorrow or regret ?
 Will they avail to give us back the
  past ?

Onward the tides of time unebbing set,
   Till on the shores of death our wrecks
     are cast.

Then let us live and love while yet we
     may,
   Nor cloud the present with the future's
     dread,
But grateful take the gift for which we
     pray,
   Content to have each day our daily
     bread.

She. Give this poem to me, and I will
keep it and read it when I am old and
gray, and wear a cap, and totter about on
pleasant summer mornings in the flower
garden ; and smile and sigh over the
past, and chatter over the old times when
I was young ; and fall asleep now and
then in my easy chair in the long winter
evenings, as I sit over the fire watching
idly the flames that shoot up and die
away ; and dreaming, and moralizing,
and comparing the meanness of to-day
with the nobler spirit of the past. And
in some such mood I shall say to my
maid Annie, " Bring me that little book

bound in vellum and gold, with a gold clasp, that is in my chamber ; " for in that, among other precious relics and mementos of the past, I shall put this poem carefully away. And she will bring it, and with a little suffusion in the eyes, that obliges me to take off my spectacles and wipe them dry, I shall read this poem, and, dropping the book in my lap, say : " Ah, me ! those were happy days. Those were happy mornings under the trees," and wonder if any one now is listening, as I did then, to poems read by a young poet while the nightingales and the purling brook are singing an accompaniment to him as he reads.

He. Yes ; and perhaps you will read them when life has not gone on so far, though youth has fled, and you have become sterner and more critical, and the romance of life is over. And then you will say : " Dear me ! dear me ! what a romantic young thing I was ! It was only youth that made these poems seem worth the listening to. I should not be able to stand them now, even with the best of will." That is far more probable.

She. Well, we will wait and see.

He. I shall have taken the long journey before that time, so that I shall not be able to see ; and besides, even if I were there, you would not acknowledge the truth. You would be too kind an old lady, as you are too generous a young one. You would have something pleasant to say, even if it went a little against your conscience.

She. Yes, I hope I should. Truth with a capital T is a hard, unsympathetic kind of creature, who is always reproving and rebuking and setting us right, and is so formal and noble and stately in her high ruff. I think I probably should dodge her, as you say, if I could, or get her out of the room. But time is going, so a truce to all this forecasting. I 'm waiting for the poem.

He. One moment, just as a comment on what we were saying, a sort of preliminary overture on an old violoncello before the play begins : —

Nought is given to keep and to own :
   Life and time, love and youth hurry
      by ;
Ere we say they are ours they are flown ;
   And memory is but a sigh, —

A sigh for a phantom that 's fled,
  For a dream that we clung to and lost,
But a funeral rite for the dead
  Of which nothing remains but the
    ghost.

Our sorrows as well as our joys
  Grow dimmer as time fleets away,
And over old pains, cares, annoys,
  Faint graces of memory play.
What we mourned for with bitterest tears,
  What with anguish we wept for a
    while,
Time softens, till after long years
  Almost on its face is a smile.

She. Thank you ; it is very pretty, but
very sad.

He. Oh, don't call it pretty. If there
is anything I hate, it is that word
"pretty." It is such a condescending
and unmeaning word. It is like flinging
a stone at a poem to call it pretty.

She. I take it back ! I never said so !

He. Thank you, that will do.

She. There were two poems I saw
when you gave me your book to look
at, that were both entitled " Good-by."
What are they ?

He. Little nothings.   Not worth reading.

She. Let me judge of that, please.
What are they ?

He. Oh, I have no objection to reading them if you wish, but I assure you —

She. Oh !   Don't assure me ; read
them.

He. To hear is to obey.   This is one of
them.

Well, well !   This is the very last, last
    day
       We shall be here ;
And I shall be so glad to get away.
       Shall you not, dear ?

Yes — no — perhaps !   't is always hard
    to say
       That word — Good-by.
No place is wholly sad, or wholly gay.
       With half a sigh

We leave the dreariest place.   However
    gray,
       Dark, tempest-tossed,
Some gleams of softening light illume
    alway
       The past and lost.

And   the   mere   words, — smile, speak
    them as we may, —
    "This is the last,"
Across the darkest and the brightest day
    A cloud will cast.

A consecrating hand time seems to lay
    On all it gave.
Griefs fade, and tender lights of memory
    play
    Even o'er the grave.

She. Yes ; there is some truth in that. Even over the dreariest and most commonplace of days and experiences that are gone there lingers a certain light, — perhaps of amusement, if of nothing else, that softens in memory all the harshness of fact and reality. We at least can laugh at what is past, however annoying and disagreeable it might have been at the time.   But now for the other poem, which I suppose is on the same lines, with a little variation, perhaps.

He. Not precisely. It is a different kind of Good-by.

She. Well, read it, please.

He. To hear is to obey.

This is the last time we shall walk to-
    gether ;
    So it all ends !
Still, if love binds us not with its strong
    tether,
    We may at least be friends.

Ah ! so you say ! but after the sweet
    hoping
    Of what might be,
Friendship sounds cold, — so cold ! In
    heaven's wide coping
    Love's light is gone for me.

Its glory gone, that once with radiant
    splendor
    Before me shone ;
With only twilight friendship, sad,
    though tender,
    To light life's journey on.

No ! I will say no more. 'T is all past
    saying.
    Here it all ends !
You know too well what on my heart is
    weighing,
    So let us part, — mere friends.

She. Yes, it is difficult to put up with second best in all cases, but specially in love, where not to be first is to be nowhere. So I imagine, at least; I never tried it. Undoubtedly you have, as you speak so feelingly about it.

He. If you suppose all these verses of mine are founded upon personal experiences, permit me to say that you are mistaken. But one may fall in love with imaginary as well as real persons, and the loss is about the same.

She. Are not many real persons purely imaginary? In fact, are not all to a certain extent in this category, — particularly when one is what we call in love? What do we really know of anybody else; nay, I might ask, even of ourselves? Of those who are nearest and dearest how little we know! Each is alone in his or her intimate individuality. However closely we may seem to be united, even in our affections and in our sympathies and feelings, still there is an impassable gulf between us. We talk of being one, but we are always two.

He. That is what I have tried to say, but, I confess, not very successfully, in these lines : —

Close at your side,
And yet as distant, dearest, each from
     each
As if some ocean, desolate and wide,
Parted our souls ; o'er which no subtlest
     speech,
No tenderest tone, look, thought, of love
     can reach,
And that abyss between us overstride.

So near, so dear,
And yet so far apart !   Each so alone
   In its deep inner life, thought, hope,
     pain, fear,
Each to the other soul so dimly known.
Each, starlike, bounded by a silent zone,
   And powerless to o'erstep its own fixed
     sphere.

Ah, to be one,
Both merged in one, not ever, ever two !
   One only ; not in earthly sense
     alone,
But soul to soul incorporate through and
     through ;
One throbbing pulse of life in me and
     you,
   One pulse of death, when this brief life
     is done.

She. Well, I don't think I could go so far as that last verse would go, for it would be only losing one's self, after all, and the bliss of loving, I should think, would be the reciprocation of the two, — of the I and thou and the thou and I, — and not the loss of all individuality. While there are two there is the charm of accord, the two tones blending into harmonies of hope, love, joy, and fear; otherwise there would be no chance of concord.

He. And none of discord, and that is something you will admit, though of very rare occurrence, — between husband and wife, at least, if not between lovers.

She. Well, I suppose you know. I give it up. I am so very ignorant of all such matters. Still, I prefer to be myself, and I don't know what sort of an unsatisfactory mixture I should make if I were identified with any other being. Ah, no! no unison for me! Concord and harmony of different tones is far better, and for myself, I 'd rather be a single note. But you see I am not a poet, and not wildly in love.

He. I dare say it is all very extravagant, but persons are so very, very extravagant when they are in love ! You must not take what they say to the letter. They are always *dying* for this and for that impossible thing. They never saw or felt anything half so perfect and so divine as everything is. When it comes to analyzing their extravagant expressions, and submitting them to the touchstone of reality, they cannot stand the test ; but to them there never was so perfect a moonlight night, nor so glorious a summer day, as every day and every night is, or so they say. They live in a dream, and a dream is generally very far removed from all the realities of life. In a dream we say and we do the most wonderful things, all of which seem to us natural, but which are in fact mere inconsecutive nonsense, for the most part at least. But dreams are dreams, for all that.

She. Sometimes I think that the world is only a dream, and we wake up when we die, as we do from our other dreams here. However, don't let us go into that question. Let us draw back our feet at once from it. And to change the subject, let me ask you if you have ever painted this delightful spot.   If you have not, you ought to.   You might put your two lovers here.

He. Will you give me a sitting for one of them ?

She. I ?   I think so !   How absurd ! But, jesting apart, have you ever painted this spot, with its mossy rocks and boulders, through which the clear running stream finds its murmurous way, spreading out into clear brown pools of transparent water now and then, in which the overhanging trees and the blue sky beyond are so softly mirrored ?   I should think you might make a charming picture of it.   You have painted it, have n't you ?

He. Yes and no.   I have tried, but I have not succeeded.   How could I succeed in rendering beyond the facts the somewhat that haunts it like a spirit ? Even the best representation of it on canvas must necessarily lack so much that the eye cannot see, but that reaches all the other senses, — the odors, the sounds, the whispering of the lightly lifting breeze among the trees, the murmur of the brook, the singing of the birds; these make up an essential part of the whole, and how can the deftest brush express them? The soul feels more than the eye sees. And besides, see how the whole place has changed in the hour that we have been here. It is still the same in a certain sense, and yet certainly different, in all the elements of light and shade and color and sentiment, with infinite and ever shifting details, at every moment having a different character, and representing a different mood and feeling.

She. I hear a great deal lately about the necessity of absolutely following nature in art; but what is nature? Is not the ugly as natural as the beautiful?

He. Ay, that is the great question, — What is nature? and what are we to imitate? Nature is as much a sentiment and a feeling as a congregation of facts. In the latter sense it has the same relation to art that a dictionary and a grammar have to poetry, or sounds to music. The great object for the artist is, as it seems to me, to select and subordinate the outward world that he sees to some idea, or

sentiment, or feeling, not servilely to
copy it. No literal reproduction of life
or nature, however accurate, results in
art. The spirit, the mind, the soul, must
come in to give them life and truth. We
must, of course, be grammatical ; but
after all, grammar is not poetry, however
correctly the words are arranged. There
is something infinitely beyond all this.
And, by the way, here are two poems
which touch upon this question.

She. Read them.

He.

Paint me the murmur of the brook,
   That through the forest flows,
The sealike whisperings of the pines,
   The perfume of the rose,
The tender tone, the finished song,
   That held our hearts awhile,
And then — but not till then — perhaps
   You 'll paint me Livia's smile.

Ah, no ! The auroral gleam that plays
   Across her happy face,
The beaming eye, the quivering lips,
   The lights that o'er it race,
The joy, the innocent surprise
   That springs from out the heart

And flushes o'er her radiant face,
    Defy the snare of Art.

No! Nature mocks the artist's skill;
    Her breathing life and charm
Flee from his grasp, and only leave
    Her cold and lifeless form.
Shy Beauty's ever varying shapes
    Art vainly strives to seize.
She lures us on, but at our touch
    She smiles and vanishes.

She vanishes, but leaves behind
    A promise in the air,
A sweet excitement, a fond hope,
    That charms away despair.
She lures the artist in his dreams,
    She will not set him free,
And in her bondage sweet he owns
    Life's best felicity.

She. Yes; 't is only one thing that can be taken at one time in art. But life and nature and beauty have infinite variations and allurements, following each other swiftly as the waves of the sea, and never the same for more than a moment. Which to take, that must be the question, since to take all is impossible.

He. Ah, yes ; that is the question.

She. Now for the other poem.

He. Well, this I call " Many Men, Many Minds." Nature is what we are ; we only see ourselves reflected in it. No. First I will read you a few lines expressing this thought on the part of the artist :

I have done my best ; but nothing seems
 worth the doing,
 Once it is done ;
And success is a phantom that ever
 eludes our pursuing
 And tempts us forever on.

The joy is alone in the earnest seeking
 and striving
 For what before us lies.
'T is only illusions that make life seem
 worth living,
 Not life's realities.

'T is the spirit that lends its charm to
 living and being,
 What we give alone we find,
'T is what we are that lends to the eye its
 seeing,
 The eye of itself is blind.

She. True, true, very true. Now for that other poem.

He. Well, you shall have it, if you insist. But I am afraid it is rather long for to-day.

She. No matter, read it.

He. Well, it must be the last for to-day, the very last. I scarcely have it in my heart, really and honestly, to read it to you. But none the less, here it is. If you will have it, you will! It is called, as I told you, —

MANY MEN — MANY MINDS.

A glorious day! June at its best; a
    smile
On all creation, — the pure heavens so
    blue,
So calm above; the fresh-washed leaves
    and grass
Twinkling in light; the delicate, soft
    breeze,
Lifting at intervals, and crisping o'er
The gleaming river, as it loitering glides
Through whitening willows, — all things
    at their best.

A day to wander without aim, and take
What, unasked, Nature yields to happy
    chance.

So thought the poet whom I chanced to
    meet
Under the canopy of murmurous leaves.
Stretched on the grass, beneath their
    shade, he lay,
Dreaming, and idly gazing now above,
Now down into the soft reflected world
That in the watery mirror quivering
    hung.
"What are you pondering now, my
    dreaming friend,"
I asked as I approached. With a half-
    smile,
Turning to me, he answered : "Ponder-
    ing ?
Nothing. Yes, absolutely nothing. 'T is
    enough
On such a day to feel and not to think.—
To feel, to dream, surrendered to the
    spell
Of all this infinite beauty, and to live,
Unquestioning, as live the trees and flow-
    ers,

Absorbed in nature, glad for what it
    gives.
Not toiling, spinning out a web of
    thought,
But, with the mind asleep, into the soul
Taking those dim reflections from above
That only come when, tranced in peace,
    we lie
Unconscious, and let Nature have her
    will.
From thoughtless hours thus spent our
    very thoughts
Returning have a radiance, color, light,
Transfiguring life itself to poesy.
So, in such hours, I no vain questions
    ask,
Nor trouble the deep flow of time where-
    in
My spirit swims, — not rooted like a rock,
To make a trouble there; but, drifting on,
Whither, who knows? nor ask me to
    what end.
Suffices me to be at one with all,
Though some may call it utter idleness."

That is one way to look at life, I
    thought,
A poet's way, and then I wandered on.

Along the meadows, pondering his words,
I passed a peasant. Through the fields
 he ploughed
With slow, dull steps, goading his labor-
 ing steers,
And shouting to them as he urged them
 on.
At times he paused to wipe from off his
 brow
The beaded sweat ; then to his work
 again
Sternly he bent himself.   Approaching
 him,
" A lovely day," I said.   " Ay, if it
 holds,"
He answered, looking up, and questioning
The open sky.   " 'T will bring good
 crops to serve
Our master's needs, at least ; and as for
 us
Who do the laborer's work, what mat-
 ters it
Sun, rain, wet, dry ; 't is all alike to us ;
Our wages are the same ; that 's the
 chief thing.
And for the rest, if this good weather
 holds,
It promises, at least, that we shall have

A bounteous harvest. But why hope for
    that ?
Was any season the world ever saw
Good for the farmer ? There's a curse
    on it ;
That's what I say ; that's my experience.
Pray as we will, sir, Nature always spites
Our wishes and our hopes. But I must
    work,
I have no time to talk, — your servant,
    sir ! "

Still further on I met a merchant friend,
Fresh from the city, overworn with care,
Pale, anxious, looking down upon the
    ground,
And heedless of the canticles the birds
Were singing in the branches, and the
    lark's
Long trill of song streaming along the
    sky.
Nothing to him had summer's bounteous
    gifts
Nor all its light and joy and life to say.
" Ah ! " he exclaimed, as I drew near,
    " What news ?
My papers have not come to-day. Have
    yours ?

Yes ?   What are the quotations ?   How
    are stocks ?
Ah ! You can't tell me. I was pondering,
As you came up, whether to buy at once
In the Southwesterns, or to wait a
    while.
They 're going up, I think. What do
    you say ?
You shake your head. They interest you
    not.
Ah, well, you see, I have to think of
    them.
Poor Jones, he 's gone at last ; a fortu-
    nate man,
Rich, very rich. You knew him, did you
    not ?
Have you heard what he left ? "

                   "Yes !   Everything ! —
Of all he spent his worried life to gain,
Nothing he took with him to where he 's
    gone ;
Not even an obolus for Charon's toll."

"God bless me," cried my friend ;
    "that 's an odd view.
Well, well ! This world is made of
    many minds."

I pondered, as I left him, both his hands
Plunged in his pockets, jingling there his
    coins,
Glad to be rid of him.

                Still further on,
Under the shadow of a noble oak,
I met an artist.   At his side I paused,
And craved his leave to overlook his
    work.
" I am ashamed of what I do," he said ;
" This beauty baffles me.   These dis-
    tances,
These wondrous tints and hazes and half-
    forms,
This unity as of one single chord.
Through all the myriad shapes and
    sounds and hues,
This strength, and this refinement, mock
    our powers.
Strive as we will, 't is vain.   The lark's
    far song
Gives color to the sky.   And how paint
    that ?
These passionate lifts and breathings of
    the air,
These murmurous whispering voices in
    the leaves,

These quivering shadows, this faint, dim
    perfume
That haunts the air, this brook's low,
    purling voice
Talking along the pebbles, — how paint
    these ?
Yet they are part and essence of the
    scene.
Ah, *that*, you see, no human hand can
    do.
The crude material facts alone we seize.
The unseen presence that pervades it
    all,
The soul that through all nature beats
    and thrills
And dimly calls us, — *that*, ah, that we
    lose,
For even our best of paintings all are
    dumb.

"Say Spring, for instance. Spring, —
    that little word
Means more, far more, than any brush
    can paint.
The poets have their will with words, but
    we
Are chained to facts, and the fine soul
    escapes,

And who can catch and keep it ? though,
    indeed,
Some happy spirits do, I know not how.

" Still, to pursue our Art, faltering to chase
The ideal phantom that forever flies,
Is joy enough.   What matters what we
    achieve,
The joy is in the chase.   Though Nature
    taunts,
She smiles on us at times, because we
    love,
Along our pathway scatters myriad flow-
    ers,
And sings to us a sweet perpetual song."

Saying " Farewell," I in the distance saw
Nelly and Bob playing beside the banks
Of the smooth river, — running to and
    fro,
Laughing and chattering in their childish
    glee,
And busy at their work, which was all
    play.
" What are you doing here ? " I cried to
    them.
"Sailing our ships," they cried. "Look
    there ! that 's Bob's,

And that is mine ahead.   You take one,
      too !
Here — this is yours ! "   And so I took a
      chip,
And we all sailed together, and our chips
Were argosies of price that sailed and
      sailed
To Indromina, up the wondrous shores
Of Andrapandra, till we reached at last
A strange, mysterious land of spice and
      flowers,
And giant palms, and trees weighed
      down with fruit
Delicious beyond telling ; where we
      spread
Our table in the shade of perfumed
      groves,
And ate and drank sweet and fictitious
      food.
And by and by dark tribes of kindly men
And long-haired women, beautiful to see,
Came gathering round us, bearing in their
      hands
Pearls, rubies, diamonds, emeralds ; and
      they talked
An Eastern tongue that no man ever
      heard,
And sang and played on wondrous instru-
      ments.

"And you," they cried to Bob, "shall be
our king,
And you be queen" (to Nelly) ; and to
me,
"You shall be grand Panjandrum of us
all !"
And then the air was rent with clash and
clang
Of golden trumpets, cymbals, bells, and
gongs,
And shouts of "Glory to our king and
queen !"

Alas ! 't was but the luncheon gong that
rang,
And all our wondrous world vanished to
air.

Such voyages we made with those small
chips
To unknown realms far up the land of
dreams ;
Such precious stones we found, beyond
all price,
Lying around us at our very feet,
That unto purblind eyes seemed pebbles
vile,
While through the magic world of make-
believe,

Made real with imaginative life,
I roamed an hour, — almost a child
    again.

Poet and artist he alone can be, —
So dreamed I as I wandered on alone, —
Who, in the fullness of his powers, can
    keep
The spell that Nature to the child has
    given,
And through imagination can transmute
The actual world around of common-
    place
To an ideal world in simple play.
For what is real in this world of ours
Save what the inward spirit lends to it?
All things around us are but what they
    seem,
And take their life and color from our-
    selves.

While work is only toil, it has the curse
Of Adam on it, and the ideal gates
That ope to Paradise are shut and
    barred.
When joy and love go with it, with a
    smile
The angel waves aside his flaming sword,

Flings the gates wide, and cries, "Come
    in ! Come in !
For you have learned the secret of the
    child."

And here ended the second day's reading in that delightful glen. But he gave
her another poem to read by herself,
for it was too long to read aloud. What
she thought of it I do not know, and
therefore I cannot truly say. Not that
I would presume, in the face of so
many instances to the contrary, to insist
that it is necessary to know before you
say — anything.

However, whatever the poem was, you
can judge for yourself, for here it is : —

A PASSING CLOUD.

He. What is it, dear ?
She.   We are alone, at last !
Why did they stay so long ? I am so
    tired
I know not what I 've said this last half
    hour.
He. Yes ; and I too am glad to be
    alone.

I 've had enough, — more than enough,
    in fact.
  She. What were you saying all that
    long, long time
You sat in the far corner with Adele,
Hidden behind the oleanders there,
Beyond the reach of ears, — almost of
    eyes ?
  He. But not of yours, at least.
  She.   No ! not of mine,
For I was curious, very. What on earth
Could you be saying to her all that time ?
  He. Saying ? Mere nothings. I can
    scarce recall
What we were saying. Compliments, of
    course ;
One has to give them to your sex, you
    know,
When they are pretty, — or they think
    they are.
They all are fond of bonbons.
  She.   By her face
I saw you lavished compliments enough,
And more than that, or so at least it
    looked.
  He. What do you mean ?
  She.   You know as well as I.
  He. I ? I know nothing. What I said
    to her

I scarce remember, — what one says to
 all.

 She. Oh, no ! Your memory 's not so
  short as that.

Think ! Think ! She blushed at first,
  and looked so pleased ;

And then the talk of both grew serious

And more than serious. Tell me what
  she said.

 He. Oh, at the last, you mean.
  Guess !

 She.   Guess, indeed !

How can I guess ?

 He.   Suppose it was of you ?

 She. Oh, Alfred ! What a —

 He.   On my faith it was.

At first I praised her dress ; then she
  praised yours,

And said how well you looked, how good
  you were,

And how she loved you. Then a story
  long

About old times she told, when you were
  girls,

Years, years ago.

 She.   And was that really all ?

 He. Yes ; really all.

 She. And you ? What did you say ?

He. I ? Say ? If I remember right, I
  said
Yes ! Certainly ! Of course ! Just like
  her ! Yes !
She always was so !   Charming, was n't
  it ?
And many another phrase as eloquent.
  She. Ah ! now you 're laughing at me.
  He.   On my word
I 'm telling you the plain, unvarnished
  truth.
What could I say but give my heart's
  consent
To all the charming things she said of
  you ?
I might have been a little shy, perhaps,
For praises of one's wife are half the
  same
As praises of one's self, since both are
  one;
Or ought to be, at least —
  She.   Yes, ought to be !
But are they ?
  He.   Very rarely, I confess.
  She. We are exceptions, then, if we
  are one.
I hope we are exceptions.
  He.   And I know
We are so, dearest —

She. Dearest ! Ah, you say
Dearest, and what a world that word
contains !
But am I really dearest ? Tell me now,
Frankly, without concealment or dis-
guise,
If still you love me as you loved me once.
I know not how I shall bear it if you say
You do not, and of course you 'll say you
do,
Whether you do or not.

He. Then where 's the use
Of asking me ?

She. Because I must, must know,
And I shall know it by your voice, face,
tone,
Whatever you may say. Oh ! look at
me,
And say, as once you said, a year ago, —
A little year, — With all my heart and
soul
I love you.

He. Why, of course, of course, I do !

She. Of course ? And why of course ?
Is that the way
To say you love me ? Ah ! 't is as I
feared.
I see it all.

He.   What do you see or fear ?
What have I said or done that thus
    point-blank
You ask me if I love you ?   Have I not
Told you a hundred times, as now again
I tell you, that I love you ?
    She.   Yes ; but not
As now you say it.
    He.   Ay ; but ne'er before
As now have you demanded in such tone
My love.   Is it an accusation now ?
    She. An accusation ?
    He.   Yes ; for it implies
Something or said, or done, or left un-
    done,
Some fault, or some neglect, I know not
    what,
Of which I have been guilty.   What is it ?
    She. I do not know.   I only see and
    feel
There is a difference.   No ! You cannot
    say
As once you said, " I love you."   That
    is why
I ask you if you love me — really —
    He. That is a question one should
    never ask,
For one should know it without asking it.

She. Well! Still I ask it, for I fear!
I fear!

He. You are too foolish, dearest. You
must know
I love you.

She. No! It will not do. You see
It will not do. You could not say it thus
If you did really love me.

He. Nor could you
Ask such a question and in such a way.
For there is nothing numbs, and hurts,
and kills,
Or, let us say, that brushes off the bloom
Of tender, delicate love, like the rude
touch
Of such suspicion. Love should not sus-
pect,
But should believe, trust, feel beyond all
doubt,
Beyond all question. Doubt divides and
chills.
When confidence departs, love spreads its
wings,
As if at least it purposed to take flight,
Whether it flies or not.

She. And if one sees
Love lift and shake its wings, one should
not cry,

Ah! Are you going?

He.   Never ! If it goes,
It goes. Such questions are not to be
    asked.
She. What should we do, then ?
He.   As Cordelia did,
" Love and be silent." If it goes, it goes.
What can prevail to stay it from its
  · flight ?
Questions ? Recriminations ? Jealous-
    ies ?
  She. How can I help being jealous?
    Yes, in truth
I am jealous, jealous of the very air.
I would have all of you, — the very all,
Not part and share with others, even
    though
The best you gave me. All ! I have
    given all,
I would have all. 'T is different with you.
All men are different, I suppose, from us.
You have so many second-bests ; but we
Have but one best, and that lost, all is
    lost.
  He. So I suppose the lover, if, in truth,
He really loves, all friendship should ab-
    jure,
Being second-bests ; should flee society
To worship only at one single shrine.

She. I think you men have all of you
    half-hearts.

He. When we give half, then we have
    given all.

What can you ask for more ?

She.   I ask no more.

Forgive me, I will try to be content.

Only I thought — No matter what I
    thought ;

You would not understand me, if indeed

I understand myself. Count all unsaid

That I have spoken. I was foolish,
    wrong ;

But when one fears to lose what is one's
    life,

'T is hard to be wise, prudent, and, in-
    deed,

Even sensible, at all times. 'T is my
    love

That makes me jealous. Let us say no
    more.

Go back and flirt with any and with
    all,

And I will strive to trust you utterly.

But smile now. Say that you forgive
    me ! No !

Not with that face, that tone, in that cold
    way !

Oh, I'm so sorry, dearest, so ashamed ;
But still I could not help it ; could not
    live
While éven a breath of doubt was on my
    faith.
Let us forget it all.
   He.   I wish I could.
'T is easy enough to say, I will forget.
To do so is not always in our power,
Even with the best of will, — but to for-
    give,
Ah, that is really easy ; and, besides,
What is there to forgive ?   Nothing at
    all.
I'm sorry that you doubted me, but still
'T was in your nature, and you spoke it
    out,
And that was honest, true, and frank,
    like you ;
Better than keeping it hid out of sight
To breed and poison all your secret
    thoughts.
So let us think no more of it.
                          How sweet
These roses smell ! and in the opal sky
There's not a cloud. Yes, one, a pale,
    thin rack
That even now is melting into air.

She. Ah, you were always, always gen-
erous.
Will you go with me in the garden now ?
The moon is at its full. On such a night,
'Twas June, as you remember, and the
air
Was faint with perfume, thrilling to the
bursts
Of hidden nightingales that, all unseen,
Poured forth their pulsing passion to the
night ;
When — Ah ! you know what happened
then, — that hour
Of overwhelming feeling that entranced
The world around us, bearing us away
Above the real to ideal realms,
Beyond all telling, — with a torrent's
force,
Sweeping us on, on, on, to where, to
what,
We knew not, thought not, cared not.
Silently,
Reft of all will, we gave ourselves to
fate,
And fate was love, and you were all in
all
To me, as I to you. That night of
nights,

That hour of hours, while life and sense
      remain,
Come what come may, we never shall
      forget.
  He. Let us, then, live it over now once
      more.
  She. Say what you said then. Do as
      then you did !
Be mine again as then you were ; no
      thought
Within your heart but me, no wish for
      more
Than I could give, did give ; for what I
      gave
Was my whole heart, that nevermore in
      life
I can take back. 'T is yours, forever
      yours.
Never in life ?   No !   Never even in
      death.
For what were heaven without you, my
      own love !
And oh, forgive me !   In your heart you
      know
'T is my deep love that wants, and longs,
      and craves,
And must have all, — oh, more than I
      deserve,

So much more — *that* is nothing ; that,
    indeed,
Is simply nothing. What I want is all ;
I cannot share you. In your love I live ;
It is the very air my soul must breathe,
Or else I die.

    He.   Who could resist you, dear ?
Not I, indeed ! my own beloved wife.

    She. Then you do love me ?

    He.   Ah, too well you know
I love you, and how deeply you may
    guess
From what you feel yourself ; but then
    you see
I cannot say it, cannot pour it forth
In words, in tones, like yours.

    She.   You did that night.
Ah, then your very soul was on your lips.
You took me as an angel takes a spirit,
And bore me up to heaven.

    He.   One cannot live
Always at heights like that. The truest
    love
With time grows calmer, stiller, not less
    deep.

    She. Colder, perhaps.

    He.   No ; if an angel came
To serve us, live with us, we could not
    bow

In endless adoration ; *that* at last
Would spoil all earthly living.   We
   should joy
With heartfelt gladness and content to
   see
Her happy smile, her gentle charm, her
   grace,
Her perfectness, and feel that it was
   ours.
We should o'erlook the angel in the wife,
And for the comfort, help, and cheer she
   lent,
Give voiceless blessing, — that we could
   not speak ;
But if beyond the simple human ways
She claimed an attitude of constant
   prayer
And humble adoration, that at last
Would tire out love, and simply ruin
   life.
  She. And is it this you think I crave of
     you ?
  He. Of course not. What I mean is,
     in this life
We must not ask too much, nor make
   ourselves
The gauge of others, even of those we
   love,

Thinking what we ourselves would say
    or do,
If left by them unsaid, undone, would
    mean
All it would mean in us. Much is un-
    said,
However deeply felt ; much left undone
Through simple carelessness. Some
    must express
All that they feel, and even go beyond
Into excess, perhaps ; while others hide
Out of pure shyness what lies deep with-
    in,
Hiding it as a miser hoards his gold.
   She. And so you think that I am one
    of those
Who overstate, exaggerate, while you
Keep silence, understate, and hide your
    thoughts ?
   He. Something like that I offer as ex-
    cuse
For my shortcomings. You 've a kind-
    lier power
Of pouring all your heart out into words.
   She. Words ? Only words ?
   He.   No, no ! Not only words.
'T is real all to you. Your eager love
Springs like a fountain up into the sun,

And frankly showers its blessing and de-
    light ;
Mine, like a runnel coursing under-
    ground,
Steals out of sight, not caring to be seen.
'T is my fault, 't is my nature. Yours,
    you see,
Is gladder, brighter, better every way.
Even now, you see, I cannot say to you
What lies within my heart, strive as I
    may.
But trust me when I say, with all my
    heart
I love you.

  She.   Oh, my dearest, first, and best,
My only love, forgive me.   I indeed
Am such a fool ; but oh, I love you so
I cannot share a tittle of your heart
With any other, scarcely in the way
Even of friendship, saving for a man.

  He. Well ! We are friends now, are
    we not ?

  She.   What ? Friends ?
That is too cold a word ; too bleak a
    word ;
That is the stalk, and not the flower of
    love.
I want the perfect flower.

He. You shall have both.
Hark! There's the nightingale again.
He knows!
To him great nature gave the power to say
I love you, with that utterance full and
rich
And passionate as none else have save you.
I can but caw and twitter at the best.
She. You are the dearest, truest, best
on earth!
He. Far from it; but no matter. I at
least
Am true to you. But, dear, 't is growing
late,
And you are tired. Shall we now go in?
She. Tired? Oh, no! Go in? Oh,
no, not yet!
I only wish this night would last forever!
Oh, I'm so sorry, so ashamed; and yet
So glad, oh, so unutterably glad!
Tell me again you love me, and again,
Again, again, a hundred thousand times;
And bid time stop and listen while you
say it;
And let the stars, trees, flowers, all earth,
all heaven,
Keep record of those dear and blessed
words!